AWAKENED BY THE SHEIKH

DESERT ROYALS

MOLLIE MATHEWS

Blue Orchid
PUBLISHING

AWAKENED BY THE SHEIKH

THE SHEIKHS UNTAMED BRIDES

MOLLIE MATHEWS

ABOUT THIS BOOK

The first book in the Desert Royals series

Awakened by the Sheikh— a forbidden love romance with royalty, redemption, and a celestial destiny written in the stars.

In a kingdom ruled by ancient stars and modern secrets, Awakened by the Sheikh is a sweeping prequel romance of hidden identity, sovereign desire, and soul-deep recognition.

Celeste Valente, a brilliant Italian astrophysicist betrayed by her peers and exiled from the career she once loved, journeys to the desert kingdom of Qamar with one mission—to disappear. But destiny has other plans.

At the unveiling of the royal observatory, Crown Prince Zayad al-Rami glimpses her in a moment of wonder—one that sparks not just his curiosity, but a magnetic pull he can't explain. She is not merely a scientist. She is a mirror of everything he has buried: awe, ache, and the desire to choose love over legacy.

But love in Qamar is not simple.

Tropes include:

🌙 Grumpy x sunshine

👑 Royalty & commoner

🏛 Forced proximity

🖤 Slow-burn emotional intimacy

❗ He falls first—but she won't trust her heart easily

As tradition, power, and politics collide, Celeste and Zayad are drawn into a quiet revolution—one that begins with stargazing and ends in the possibility of reshaping an empire.

PROLOGUE

Italy, 34 years earlier

Celeste Valente was five years old the first time she tried to catch a star.

It was the summer after her parents had stopped coming to visit. No one said it aloud, but their absence lingered like perfume after the person has gone—untraceable and heavy. She had asked once, timidly, if they'd be coming to her birthday. Her grandmother had paused, mid-stitch, and said only, "Not this year, amore. They are... far away."

So that evening, barefoot in the courtyard of her grandmother's old villa in the hills above Florence, Celeste pressed her tiny palms to the warm stone tiles and whispered a secret to the sky. If her parents wouldn't come down to her, maybe the stars would.

The courtyard smelled of lemons and sun-warmed jasmine. The air buzzed with cicadas hidden in the olive trees. It should have been a night like any other—but something in her heart told her it wasn't. Something in the quiet seemed to listen.

"Nonna," she asked, standing on tiptoe, her little night-dress fluttering at her knees, "where do the stars go when the sun comes up?"

Her grandmother looked up from her embroidery, moonlight softening the fine lines around her eyes. "They don't go anywhere, tesoro mio. They're always there. You just can't see them in the light."

Celeste squinted up at the night sky, as if trying to catch them before they could vanish again. "But why would something so beautiful hide?"

A pause. Her grandmother's needle stilled in the fabric.

Then—very gently—she set the hoop aside and opened her arms. Celeste crawled into her lap, nestling against the crinkly fabric of her linen blouse, the smell of lavender soap and something older—something warm and familiar—surrounding her like a lullaby.

"They don't hide," Nonna murmured into her hair. "The sun just outshines them for a while. But when darkness returns, they're still waiting—right where you left them. Like secrets that only show themselves when you're quiet enough to listen."

Celeste held her breath. The stars above blinked down at her, winking secrets she could almost—but not quite—understand. One twinkled a little brighter than the others. She stretched out her fingers, reaching as high as she could. But it stayed far above her reach, a drop of fire she could only feel with her heart.

She didn't make a wish that night.

She made a promise.

Someday, she told the star silently, I'll find you. I'll know where you go when no one sees you. I'll understand why beautiful things disappear. And I'll never stop looking, even when everyone else tells me to give up.

In the years to come, when people tried to put her in a box, when they called her strange or too curious or too stubborn, she would remember that moment under the stars.

She would remember the weight of her grandmother's arms, the ache in her chest she didn't have words for, and the glow in the sky that never truly left.

It would be years before she would learn how to name grief.

Even longer before she realized she had always been waiting for something more than answers.

She had been waiting to return to the light.

And someday, she would.

Even if it meant reaching for a star she couldn't trust.

Even if it meant standing beside a man she couldn't quite believe.

Even if it meant remembering how to love herself first.

CHAPTER ONE

The Royal Observatory Dome, Emirate of Qamar

Crown Prince Zayad Al-Rami did not believe in fate. But something shifted the night he first saw her.

The gala was just another obligation—another polished evening of veiled agendas wrapped in diplomacy and champagne. The Royal Observatory Dome shimmered under soft golden light, its centuries-old stone and iron latticework transformed into a theatre of modern invention. Telescopes stood like silent sentinels beneath the open sky, and the air carried the scent of jasmine, sand, and ambition.

He loathed these events, where science was paraded like a prized falcon, leashed and displayed for the benefit of men who understood little and invested even less. But the observatory was his grandfather's legacy. And so, he showed his face.

He had intended to stay for one hour.

Until he saw her.

A woman as radiantly beautiful as a star. She stood apart from the crowd, half-hidden behind the telescope on the western balcony. A linen shawl draped over her shoulders, understated, elegant. Her ebony hair was pinned up in a way that revealed the curve of her neck, though rebellious strands had slipped free, curling with the breeze like they refused to be tamed.

She wasn't trying to be noticed.

Which is exactly why he couldn't stop looking.

Zayad narrowed his gaze. There was something coiled about her stillness, something self-contained. Her eyes—he couldn't see the color yet, but he saw how they moved, not scanning the room like a guest, but the stars above like a pilgrim searching for signs.

Someone murmured near him.

"Dr. Celeste Valente. Visiting from Europe. The astrophysicist."

The name stirred something.

He remembered the controversy—years ago, a scandal in scientific journals. A promising researcher whose groundbreaking model of the universe had been credited to a male colleague. Her protests had been silenced as conspiracy, false information, ungrounded in fact. There had been no trial, no defense—only her disappearance from the field's center stage.

Until now.

Zayad excused himself from the ambassador's circle and made his way toward her, deliberate but unhurried. She glanced at him when he approached—calm, unreadable, her posture measured and reserved.

"You're not like the others," he said, his voice low, deliberate. "You stand apart."

She turned her head slowly, eyes narrowing with an edge of amusement. "Is that supposed to be a compliment... or a warning?"

He met her gaze evenly. "Neither. Just an observation."

A flicker passed across her features—evasive, unreadable. Then the corner of her mouth tugged, just slightly. Not quite a smile. More like a challenge wrapped in stardust. And just as quickly, it disappeared.

She didn't reward men easily. He respected that.

They didn't waste breath on small talk. Not with the night pressing in so thick with meaning. Instead, they spoke of dark energy. Gravitational collapse. The peculiar loneliness of neutron stars. It should have felt abstract, academic—but with her, it was electric. Alive.

Her brilliance wasn't rehearsed. It hadn't been polished for performance. It carried scars. The kind of intelligence forged in silence, in solitude. She spoke like someone who had once believed the world would listen—and learned the cost when it didn't. Now, she only offered words when they carried weight.

That, more than anything, fascinated him.

Above them, the dome's hatch began to creak open, the crowd rustling with anticipation. Light spilled down in a single, focused beam.

Applause broke the quiet.

But Zayad didn't look at the telescope.

He looked at her.

Her face turned upward, eyes fixed on the emerging stars. And for a moment—just a moment—something unguarded cracked through.

He saw it in her stillness.

Not awe, exactly. But reverence. As if the stars weren't objects to study, but old friends returning home. There was a softness in her then, delicate and aching, like a memory being pulled gently to the surface.

She didn't need to possess the stars.

She remembered them.

And in that single, soul-lit instant, Zayad—who had negotiated peace treaties, buried his own heart, and stood unshaken before kings—felt something ancient shift inside him.

Not desire.

Recognition.

This was not a woman who would ever orbit another's gravity.

And yet, he knew—he would spend the rest of his life resisting the pull of hers.

Or surrendering to it completely.

CHAPTER TWO

C eleste preferred mornings before the city woke.

Before the hum of traffic returned, before the air grew thick with ambition and perfume and noise.

She sat at the small cedar writing desk in her apartment overlooking the walled gardens of the institute. The first call to prayer had come and gone. The sun hadn't yet crested the rooftops, and a silvery haze hovered over the desert hills in the distance.

Her coffee sat untouched. She stared at the blank page of her journal, her pen resting between her fingers like a conductor waiting for the right note.

It had been years since she'd opened this one—the deep blue leather-bound notebook embossed with a tiny constellation on the cover. Her Star Journal, she once called it. A private record of skies seen, questions whispered to the stars, moments measured not in time but in presence.

She had stopped writing in it the day the sky betrayed her. Or rather, the world of science did.

She remembered it too clearly: the scandal that erupted

across journals and conferences. Her groundbreaking cosmological model—an elegant reframing of dark energy dynamics—had been leaked and published under the name of a male colleague. One she had trusted.

When she spoke up, the institutions turned their telescopes the other way. Her name was redacted. Her claims dismissed as conspiracy, unprofessional, "unsubstantiated."

There was no formal trial. No hearing. Just silence. And her slow erasure from the field she had once called home.

She had walked away. Not from the stars. But from the people who claimed to measure them.

Since then, the journal had remained closed.

But now, as the desert light crept through the blinds and brushed the corner of the page, something stirred. Not forgiveness—not yet. But the faint glimmer of something just as fragile: a return.

Celeste pressed her pen to the paper.

And for the first time in years, the stars had something to say.

Last night…

She drew a breath, then pressed pen to paper.

13th Sha'ban, under a waxing crescent
Observation: Anomaly detected in social atmosphere.
Unexpected gravitational event.
Subject identified as Crown Prince Zayad Al-Rami.

She hesitated. Even writing his name felt dangerous. Not because he was dangerous, though she hadn't ruled that out, but because the way he unsettled her was not rooted in fear.

Encounter occurred at the Royal Observatory Dome during
the inaugural gala. Subject entered orbit unannounced. No

grand display. No predictable pattern. Initial visual analysis:
composed, restrained, unreadable.
But beneath the surface... charged.

She tapped the pen against her chin.

There was something elemental about him. The kind of man who didn't need to raise his voice because the silence around him carried weight. He hadn't tried to impress her. He hadn't asked questions. He had simply stood there, fully present, fully watching.

His words were sparse, intentional. Like dropped stones in still water.

Observed no signs of ego-driven velocity.
No attempt to diminish or dominate.
Unexpected.

What unnerved her most was the moment the dome opened.

The crowd had turned their eyes upward in awe, but hers had met the sky already—as always.

Only this time, she had not been alone in her wonder.

When she glanced sideways, she found his gaze fixed not on the stars, but on her.

Not with possession.

Not desire.

But recognition.

It startled her more than if he'd touched her.

He stood beside her, tall and unwavering, his presence like something forged from ancient stone and flame. Zayad Al-Rami—Crown Prince of Qamar, commander of armies, sovereign of silence.

The kind of man empires didn't just follow—they anticipated.

Moonlight gilded the edges of his profile—sharp cheekbones, a sculpted mouth, and eyes the color of obsidian, fathomless and watching. His body, honed and regal beneath desert silk, radiated a stillness so potent it made everything else seem noisy.

But it wasn't his beauty that unsettled her.

It was his gravity.

He looked at her like she was a constellation only he could see clearly. And something in her—something buried under layers of protocol, disappointment, and self-preservation—shifted in return.

As if he saw something even she had forgotten.

Hypothesis: Subject may operate according to an unfamiliar kind of gravity. One that does not pull or force, but listens.
Waits.
Caution: Field remains unstable. Approach with care.
Conclusion: Data insufficient. Further observation required.

She closed her notebook slowly, her fingers lingering on the cover.

It wasn't the attraction that shook her. She'd felt that before. Been burned by it, deceived by the way admiration could be mistaken for understanding.

No, this was different.

This felt like the desert stars.

Distant. Quiet. Alive.

And if you stood still long enough—really still—they began to speak.

She wasn't sure what they were saying yet.

But she knew one thing.

She wanted to listen.

Celeste pushed back from the desk and finally took a sip of her coffee. It had gone cold.

She didn't care.

Something warm was already moving inside her.

Something ancient.

Something unnamed.

It curled at the edges of her reason, whispering promises she wasn't ready to hear. Not yet.

She snapped the journal shut with a little more force than necessary.

Whatever that pull was—she would chart it, study it, survive it.

But she would not surrender to it.

Not now.

Not here.

Not for a man who looked at her like she was already his.

She would keep watching.

But she wouldn't fall.

Not unless the stars themselves commanded it.

CHAPTER THREE

Later that week, an envelope was slipped under the door of her office at the Qamar Institute. The envelope was thick, the paper cream-colored and edged in gold. No return address, no crest—just her name in calligraphy that made her breath catch.

Dr. Celeste Valente.

She turned it over in her hands, fingertips tingling with the echo of something ceremonial. The kind of invitation that felt less like an offer and more like a threshold.

She slit the seal open carefully and unfolded the single card inside.

You once said you longed to fly through the stars.
Aldebaran rises next week—bright and unchallenged. A
caravan will depart from the southern gate at dusk.
If you wish to come, bring nothing but time.
And your eyes.
— Z

She read it twice. Then again.

Aldebaran.

The red eye of Taurus.

The star that had guided caravans, kings, and seekers across desert sands for millennia.

Even ancient astrologers had revered it as one of the four Royal Stars—the Watcher of the East.

It was said to guard doorways between worlds. A harbinger. A witness.

And Sheikh Zayad wanted her to see it with him.

Not from a rooftop. Not from an observatory.

But from a place where time hadn't broken the sky, a sacred desert site whispered about among the old scholars, half-legend, half-myth.

She rose from her desk, heart pounding, the card still clutched in her hand.

Why her?

He hadn't tried to contact her since the gala. No follow-up. No pressure. Just that one night of stargazing and a silence that felt less like distance and more like invitation.

And now… this.

She moved to her window and looked out over the gardens. In the distance, the desert shimmered beneath the late afternoon light, pale gold and endless. The idea of leaving the city, even for a night, unsettled her. Her routines were protective. Familiar. Safe.

But Aldebaran had always been more than a star to her.

As a girl, she had traced its burnished glow with her fingertips on star charts, whispering its name like a prayer. Even now, the thought of seeing it from a place untouched by artificial light, surrounded by the silence of dunes, pulled at her like gravity.

And Zayad…

He had chosen that star.

He understood its significance.

Not just astronomically. But spiritually. Symbolically.

He was speaking to the part of her she kept hidden.

The part that still believed the stars were sacred.

She pressed the invitation to her chest and let her eyes close for a moment.

She didn't know what awaited her in that desert.

But she knew this:

If she didn't go, she would never forgive herself.

CHAPTER FOUR

The caravan departed just after dusk, travelling the road to Aldebaran – Rub' al Khali.

Six camels, robed guides in indigo veils, two low-slung lanterns swaying at the lead, and silence more eloquent than speech. Celeste had been told nothing beyond the time to arrive and what to bring: nothing but time, and her eyes.

She wore loose linen in moon-washed hues, her hair braided down her back, her journal tucked close in a leather satchel. She had never ridden a camel before, but the sway of its gait quickly became rhythm—lulling, strange, oddly comforting.

The city vanished behind them like a mirage. Ahead: dunes. Endless. Undisturbed. The sky deepened from cobalt to indigo, stars emerging one by one like secrets coming to light.

She didn't speak. Neither did the others.

Somewhere near the front of the procession, Zayad rode in silence, his silhouette sharp against the horizon—cloak billowing, head turned skyward every so often, as if listening to something older than time.

The air cooled. Sand whispered. A warm breeze tugged at her scarf.

Above her, the sky bloomed.

The stars out here were not the same as those she charted on paper or tracked through observatory glass. They pulsed. They shimmered with intent. The Milky Way arched over-head, a river of light pouring across the heavens. Planets shimmered like drops of molten metal, and constellations she had memorized since childhood now looked new, reborn in the absence of human interference.

And then, like a slow exhale from the winter sky, Alde-baran rose above the eastern dunes. Blood-orange and unblinking. Watching.

A red jewel. A steady, pulsing fire.

The Eye of the Bull.

Celeste's breath caught in her throat.

It was brighter than she remembered. Larger. More alive. It hovered just above the dunes like a beacon—a celestial eye watching, knowing, waiting.

They rode toward it.

Time blurred as they rode toward it—unravelling like a spool of golden thread in the sand. Celeste no longer knew how long they had been traveling. Her thighs ached from the unfamiliar sway of the camel, her spine tender with each jolt —but she didn't care.

The night air was cool against her skin, laced with the scent of crushed sage and the faint salt of her own sweat. Her fingers curled tightly around the worn leather of her satchel, grounding her in the only thing she could hold.

Something ancient was calling her forward.

Not with sound, but with memory. With gravity.

It felt like being remembered by the Earth itself. As if the stars ahead were not distant, but waiting—watching—bowing low enough, just this once, for a woman who had dared to follow them.

And she would. Even with him. *Zayad*. Even if every step cracked her open.

She could feel his presence like heat at the edge of her awareness—steady, unspoken, impossible to ignore. It wasn't just attraction, the way her heart thundered when he looked at her, nor the tingle that scuttled up the fine hairs on her arms when his hand brushed hers. It was something deeper. More familiar. More dangerous.

A kind of recognition she hadn't expected.

She didn't want to believe in it. Not now. Not again. Not after what desire had cost her the last time.

This wasn't the kind of pull she could rationalize, decipher mathematically or reduce to chemistry. It felt like the beginnings of a constellation—lines being drawn between stars that had long thought themselves alone.

No.

She couldn't trust that.

Not now. Not ever. And yet...

She would go where the sky touched the sand—even with him in her orbit. But her heart... her heart would stay tethered to caution, unless the stars decided otherwise.

At last, the caravan crested a high dune and descended into a hollow that opened like a breath held for centuries.

The sacred site was a circle of black stones, smoothed by wind and time, surrounding a flat platform carved into the earth. Small oil lamps flickered at the perimeter, but otherwise the site was left in darkness, so the stars could reign, commanding the heavens.

Zayad dismounted first.

He did not offer his hand. He only looked at her with that same quiet knowing that had followed her since the gala. Did he know that if he rushed her she would run? Impossible. And yet...

Celeste dismounted on her own. Her legs, unused to the camel's sway, wobbled beneath her—but she straightened, refusing to show weakness. The night air kissed her flushed skin, cooling everything but the pulse of her heart pounding low and insistent.

She clasped her hands before her, the tremble in her fingers betraying the ache she couldn't speak aloud.

She wanted to kiss him.

Just once.

Perhaps then, having tasted what was forbidden, her longing would be sated. That traitorous, treacherous, tameless desire that tugged the corners of her lips, taunting, *Kiss him. Kiss him. I dare you. Prove you feel nothing for the prince of stars.*

Her eyes traced the curve of Zayad's jaw, shadowed and sharp beneath starlight. The column of his throat, bronzed and exposed where his robe parted. His hands—broad and bronzed, steady as stone, yet rough with the memory of sand and sword. The kind of hands that had commanded kingdoms... and could unfasten a woman's breath with a single touch.

It was not just his beauty. It was the stillness beneath it. The way he watched her like she was something sacred—not a woman to possess, but a force to reckon with.

She hated how deeply she felt it. How her body responded

with the instinct of someone long-starved for being seen this way.

Kiss him. Kiss him. I dare you. Prove you feel nothing for the prince of stars.

No!

She turned her eyes to the heavens. Fixed them on Alde-baran. Willed herself into the star's fire, into that unreachable place where feelings could not touch her. Where longing could not burn.

She wanted to walk into the light and disappear before this pull unraveled her.

His eyes never left hers. No command. No question.

Only offering.

Kiss him. Kiss him. I dare you. Prove you feel nothing for the prince of stars.

Just once.

Perhaps…

And then, without a word, Zayad stepped aside. She pressed her lips together, clamping down the reckless longing that had nearly claimed her caution. She might have felt rejected, but rather than refuse her silent longing, he was letting her enter the sacred circle first.

As if to say: *You are the star tonight. Not I. Not us. Not we. Just you.*

She stepped past him. Her arm brushed his. Just barely.

But it was enough.

Enough to ignite every nerve she'd tried to quiet. Enough to remind her that danger did not always come with weapons.

Sometimes it came wrapped in silence. In starlight. In the body of a man who sensed too much.

CHAPTER FIVE

Later that night, the fire crackled low, fed with slivers of cedar and desert brush that hissed sweetly in the flames. They sat across from each other on woven mats, the circle of ancient stones encircling them in quiet reverence. The rest of the caravan had withdrawn to a respectful distance, leaving only the two of them and the stars.

Aldebaran burned overhead—steady, patient, watching.

Celeste drew her shawl tighter around her shoulders, not because she was cold, but because something inside her had begun to tremble. The kind of tremble that came not from fear, but from the slow, unbearable weight of unasked questions.

She stared at the fire, then at him.

He sat easily, one knee drawn up, hands resting in the folds of his dark robe. The flames danced across the planes of his face—sharp, shadowed, beautiful. He had said little since they arrived. And yet, she had never felt more seen.

The words pressed against her throat until they could no longer be held back.

"Why did you bring me here?"

Zayad didn't answer.

She tried again, more softly this time. "Why me?"

He looked at her then, his eyes reflecting the firelight and something older—something that pulsed like gravity.

"Because you love the stars," he said simply as though that explained everything.

She laughed, but it caught in her chest, brittle. She needed more. Much more. Her cultivated aloofness was unravelling with the speed of a comet falling through the sky. She pressed on, unable to stop. "Yes… but you must know a thousand people who do. You could've brought anyone," she said with forced nonchalance, hoping he didn't detect the need in her voice. "Astronomers. Diplomats. Poets. Women—" she added, "far more graceful than me. You have palaces to run. Projects. Wars to win, for all I know. So tell me—why? I need to know why."

Zayad was quiet for a long moment.

The wind brushed across the hollow, lifting a fine drift of sand that shimmered like gold dust.

Finally, he spoke. "Because when you look at the stars, you're not trying to own them. Or explain them. You listen. You let them remain sacred."

His voice was low, but there was nothing shallow in its depth.

"I've spent most of my life surrounded by people who want to conquer light. Bottle it. Brand it. Monetize it. I've built empires alongside them. But you…" He leaned forward slightly, elbows on his knees, the firelight illuminating his face in iridescent gold, "You look at the stars the way a child looks at a miracle. And it reminded me that I used to feel that wonder, too."

Celeste didn't speak. Her throat was thick as she gazed into his eyes. Wonder. That was what he had lost and sought.

"The first time I saw you—at the gala—you didn't smile. You didn't play the game. But when that dome opened and Aldebaran rose, your face... it changed. You didn't even know you were glowing."

She looked away, trying to steady her breath. His words so earnest and sweet and...

dangerous.

"I brought you here," he said, softer now, "because the desert skies are the clearest and most awe-inspiring places to stargaze. No light pollution, dry air, and unobstructed horizons. I wanted to see if you would glow like that again. And you did. More brightly than before."

Celeste pressed her fingertips to her lips.

Oh no!

He saw beneath the mask. His words reached inside her chest and touched the most intimate part of her. The fire cracked, a log splitting gently at the heart. Somewhere deep in her chest, something gave way—something old and tightly held.

"What are you saying?" she whispered. "I don't know what to do with this,"

"*This?*"

"Your words, your kindness."

Your intimacy.

"You don't have to do anything," he said. "Just be here. Enjoy the stars."

She looked at him again. This time, she didn't look away.

"You want nothing in return."

"Just your wonder," he said.

And for the first time in years, she let herself feel the quiet ache of being chosen—not for her selflessness, not for her brilliance, not for her usefulness, nor for her beauty… but for the way her soul touched the sky.

The fire burned low.

The silence between them was no longer filled with questions.

Only recognition.

And the long, slow pull of two celestial bodies—
one born to rule,
the other born to rise—
finally, gently, defying gravity…
falling into orbit.

CHAPTER SIX

The first threads of dawn unraveled slowly across the sky, painting the desert in opal and rose. The fire had died down to soft embers, casting a warm blanket of gold over the sacred circle. The stones still radiated the heat of the night, but the air had cooled, and a hush had fallen that was deeper than sleep.

Celeste sat alone on the eastern side of the circle, her shawl wrapped loosely around her, her knees drawn to her chest. She wasn't cold, but she held herself anyway—as if anchoring something that might float away.

Zayad approached quietly, his footsteps silent in the sand.

She sensed him before she heard him.

"Aldebaran is fading," she said without turning. "Even fire must rest."

He crouched beside her, not too close, not too far. Close enough that she could feel his warmth.

"It never disappears," he murmured. "It just moves into another sky."

She turned her head to look at him then, and in the soft light, she could see the weariness in his eyes. Not from the journey, but from something much older. A life lived at high altitudes. A man born to bear weight.

There were no words left to say.

Only this moment.

Zayad reached into the folds of his robes and drew out something small. His fingers cradled it delicately, reverently. A slender leather wristband, its edges softened by time, its surface etched with constellations that glinted faintly in fading gold. He held it out in his open palm, as though it were an offering at an altar.

"It belonged to my mother," he said softly. "She called it her sky map. She wore it whenever the world felt too heavy. She said it reminded her that even in the darkest night—even after the worst betrayals—there was always a way forward. If she remembered to look up."

Celeste froze.

Her mind, trained to analyze, spun faster than her heart could catch. That what was her grandmother had told her as a child. Why Was he telling her this now? Why was he giving her this gift? Something which belonged to his mother must be far too precious to give to a stranger.

Was he trying to soften her with sentiment, to buy trust the way others had tried before—only to twist it later? Was this manipulation cloaked as something meaningful? Was he trying to tell her that she was special?

The gift itself was special. Beautiful. Intimate.

Too intimate.

She should refuse it. But how. He was the Crown Prince, and she was a visitor in his Kingdom. This was the kind of gesture that left you exposed if you took it—and foolish if you didn't. "Why are you giving it to me?" she asked, the words smaller than she intended.

"Because you carry the same light she did. That same

fierce grace." His eyes held hers, steady and certain. "My mother believed stars don't just guide us. They remember us. You're not lost, Celeste. You're just... finding your way home."

Lost.

The word landed like a stone in her gut.

Was that what he thought? That she was adrift—some helpless, broken thing searching for a place to belong?

Her jaw clenched, heat blooming behind her eyes.

She wasn't some fragile waif in need of saving. She had survived her childhood. She had climbed out of the wreckage of her career with fierce determination and a strengthened resolve to maintain her independence. She had shown she needed no one. And yet...

And yet the bracelet shimmered with a quiet ache. A stillness that didn't ask her to be anything, not strong nor soft, but who she was. Maybe she was overthinking his motivation. Perhaps he didn't see her as lost at all. Maybe he saw her as seen as his mother had been.

She reached out, her hand trembling just slightly, and took the sky map from his palm. The leather was warm from his skin. Worn. Real.

If this was a trick to make her to beholden to him in some way, so be it. He could not make her do anything she didn't want. She'd survive any fallout if she had to assert her will. But part of her—maybe the bravest part—hoped she wasn't be set up for future failure.

Her hand lifted to meet his—tentative, unsure. How many stories ended like this? A royal and a woman with desert sand in her shoes and stardust in her eyes. She wasn't of his world. She never had been. She never would be.

And yet, when her fingers brushed his, something ancient stirred between them.

Not a spark. A flame.

Not heat. Gravity.

That single touch—skin to skin, soul to soul—carried the weight of lifetimes.

Still, she hesitated.

He was raised behind palace walls, taught diplomacy and sacrifice. She was raised by stars, taught to trust no one but the sky.

She slipped the Sky Map over her wrist like armor disguised as grace. She said nothing. Words would have broken the delicate truth hovering between them. She whispered, not to him, but to herself:

This time, I won't run. This time I will fight the darkness with light.

His eyes shimmered as he looked at her, as though he had heard her silent affirmation, but she didn't look away. She didn't falter. Instead, she fastened the band around her wrist with quiet reverence. It didn't just fit—it settled there like it had been waiting across lifetimes to return. A fragment of memory. A piece of her own lost light, come home.

And maybe, somehow, it had.

In another lifetime.

In another life.

They sat in silence watching the sky as the sun rose over the dunes, bathing the ancient stones in gold. The sky blushed. The earth held its breath. And in that holy place, something passed between them.

She felt his intention before he reached for her—slowly, like the heavens had made the decision for him.

This time, I won't run. This time it is the light which will fight.

Fight to free myself from the fear of tasting him. Fight to free myself from the fear of needing him. Fight to free myself from the fear of being abandoned by him.

She met him halfway, lifting her face to his. He cupped her cheeks and lowered his mouth to hers. Their lips touched —not in haste, not in hunger, but in recognition. Like stardust finding stardust. Like constellations aligning after lifetimes apart.

Celeste lost all sense of time, falling deeper and deeper into the sweet honeyed taste of him. It wasn't just a kiss. It was a vow written in breath. A celestial collision. A surrender without words.

When they pulled apart, the air between them shimmered with everything unspoken.

A fragile beginning like a desert rose unfurling.

They didn't speak.

They didn't need to.

Because in the unspoken language of royalty and rebellion, they had already said everything. Their lives would never be the same.

CHAPTER SEVEN

A week had passed since they returned from the desert. Everything had changed. Celeste felt it in the rhythm of her breath, like her lungs had learned a new way to inhale wonder. The world shimmered, brighter than before, as if the stars they'd watched together had etched themselves into the lifelines of her palms. She caught herself smiling at nothing. Laughing too easily. Reaching for the leather band around her wrist as if it were a secret talisman—one she dared not explain.

And for a while... Zayad had orbited close. Not with grand gestures, but in the quiet ways that undid her. A lingering glance across the courtyard. A brush of fingers that made her forget her name. A silence between sentences that pulsed with unspoken promises.

Her heart, traitorous thing, had started to hope.

But then—he vanished.

Not publicly. Not fully. No, Zayad Al-Rami fulfilled every royal duty with effortless precision. Meetings, briefings, orders... all delivered with perfect poise.

But things were different between them. She knew. She felt it. The warmth was gone.

The silence between them had returned. Not the sweet silence of shared understanding, this time, it was glacial. Icy with restraint. And she had no idea why. He answered her messages with crisp formality, every word a blade. He cancelled a stargazing session he'd promised—without reason. Without remorse.

And when she passed him in the corridor of the Institute that morning, her fingers trembling from the absence of him he looked away. Too fast. Too practiced. As if even seeing her was a threat he couldn't risk.

At first, she told herself she was imagining it. Overthinking. Judging wrongly. That their kiss beneath the desert stars hadn't meant more to her than to him. That maybe she was just tired. Or hormonal. Or foolish.

But then came the gut-clenching ache.

Deep.

Aching.

Unmistakable.

And in that hopeful space in her heart where closeness had once stirred, she realized: Whatever had sparked between them beneath the stars had only been real to her. But to Zayad it meant nothing? Not any more. Whatever had passed between them was already gone.

Her mood darkended. She wanted to pack her bags and leave. Immediately. She glanced down at the Sky Map, wrapped protectively around the pulse of her wrist, and as she did the pledge she had made rose into her consciousness, blazing with fury.

This time, I won't run. This time I will fight the darkness with light.

How dare he shut her out like that. She didn't care if he

was the Crown Prince or the King of England, she deserved an explanation.

That night, she found him alone in the observatory's highest tower—his silhouette carved against the moonlit sky, hands braced on the ancient stone railing as if holding himself back from flying or falling. The desert wind tugged at his cloak like it, too, wanted answers.

She didn't call out.

He turned slowly, sensing her. His face was cast in shadow, unreadable. But his eyes—those storm-dark eyes—weren't void of feeling. They were carved with it. And pain.

"You shouldn't be here," he said quietly.

Celeste's voice held no apology. "Too late."

Silence stretched between them, tight as wire. Every second threatened to snap.

"If I've misread something," she said, stepping into the breach, "if you regret what happened in the desert—then say it." Her words were bold. Braver than her heart, which hammered with every syllable.

Zayad's jaw flexed. "I don't regret it."

"Then what's with the silent treatment?" Her voice fractured. "One moment, I'm kissing you beneath the stars. The next... you disappear like I imagined everything."

He turned away, fists curling against the stone. The muscles in his back shifted beneath the fabric of his robe like he was holding something in—something vast and dangerous.

"You don't understand," he said at last, his voice roughened by restraint.

"Then help me," she whispered, stepping closer.

His silence howled. She could feel it thrumming through the space between them.

"What don't I understand?"

He exhaled slowly.

Still nothing. She waited, meeting silence with silence. She would not beg. She would not grovel. What she would do was wait for as long as it took for him to give her an answer.

Finally he spoke. "I was raised to believe that men like me are made for glory. Command. Control. We wear power like armor and keep our hearts sealed behind duty and diplomacy." He turned to her, and his next words were barely a breath. "Because anything else... love, especially love. . .is weakness."

"Love?" she whispered, the word fragile between them.

His eyes darkened. "Love makes you fall."

The truth broke from him like confession. As if the word had cost him everything.

'Then fall,' she wanted to say, foolish, reckless and real. 'Fall with me.' The words caught in her chest. Was she deluded? How dare she even think he would fall in love with her, let alone dare to command it. She wasn't a princess. She wasn't royalty. She wasn't worthy.

She was plain Celeste, the commoner with stars in her heart and no throne to offer—only the terrifying, soul-changing hope of something real ignited by a forbidden kiss.

He closed his eyes, as if her presence hurt.

"Love is a luxury I can not afford," he said at last. "I have lost too much, My mother. My brother. My freedom to make my own choices. Everything I ever loved disappeared. Even if I could keep it, I don't know how to hold something I cannot control."

Celeste's heart didn't break for herself—it broke for him. For the boy hidden behind the crown. She had heard the whispers about the Queen's fall from favor. About his brother's rebellion. About the dangerous price of disobedience in a kingdom built on protocol and silence.

She didn't press. She didn't pry. She didn't try to wedge open the door of his grief with force. Instead, she met him there. In the silence.

Zayad's eyes opened slowly.

"The poets say men were made for glory," she murmured, her voice soft as sand shifting in wind, "but the gods kept glory for themselves. So to make men vulnerable, they gave them the gift of love. It's our superpower—our strength but also our weakness," she said, as much to herself as to him. She stepped toward him and took his hand.

"You are allowed to be human, Zayad. You are allowed to surrender. Not everything can be controlled. The stars teach us that."

He didn't answer. The armour was still there. But his fingers closed around hers.

She gazed out the window at the towering stone walls of the palace. What would it take to break these formidable towers hewn by thousands of years of duty and sacrifice? Should she even try?

CHAPTER EIGHT

That night, long after she had descended the observation tower, Celeste's thoughts refused to settle.

She sat by her window, journal unopened on her lap, the constellations embossed on the cover catching the moonlight like a memory. Her fingers brushed the leather band on her wrist—the one he had given her—and she found herself asking a question she hadn't dared voice aloud in years:

When did I decide to hide?

Not just my feelings. Not just my fears.

But my light.

My brilliance.

My voice.

My sovereignty.

My right to be loved, regardless of class or gender or race. Not because I was born to rule, or belonged in one special place, but because I existed.

She thought back to her Star Journal and the very first entry, written by starlight as a child in her grandmother's courtyard. *Where do the stars go during the day?* she had asked. And her grandmother, Nonna had said, They don't go anywhere. The light just hides them for a while.

And just like that, Celeste remembered. There had been a time when she didn't hide. A time before her parents abandoned her. Before institutions stole her ideas. Before colleagues stole her credit. Before men praised her mind but recoiled from her fire.

A time when the stars didn't feel so far away and she believed her light could guide her way.

And now… Zayad's touch, his kiss, his confession—had awakened that same aching need again—to be loved without walls. Perhaps he had been right when he said she was lost. She had lost the belief that she was lovable. Not just because of her parents' abandonment. But because she had convinced herself she was unworthy. If she had been stronger, she wouldn't have allowed herself to be betrayed. She would have fought for her rightful position. But what did the past have to do with her feelings for Zayad? Had their paths crossed because he was there to teach her what the stars had been unable to persuade her?

Teach her what? To stop hiding in daylight. To stop believing that her light had to be dimmed? To stop settling for less than she dreamed?

But that dream came with danger. Real, political, emotional.

And even as she felt herself drawn to him—despite everything—she knew even if they could be together, his kingdom would be opposed.

She wasn't ready to fight. She wasn't ready to fall.

Not yet.

Not until she remembered how to rise.

So she opened the journal. Slowly. And wrote, for the first time in years:

The stars are still there.
I'm just learning how to see myself among them again.

She closed the journal softly, the weight of the pen still warm in her hand.

The words sat on the page like stars reappearing after a long eclipse.

And then, almost without thinking, she wrote another line beneath them:

When I learn to love myself again—fully, fiercely, without apology—when I let myself shine like a star, fearless and unhidden, perhaps then… I will be ready to risk my heart.

Zayad had said love made men weak. But the ache in her chest wasn't just heartbreak—it was recognition. A familiar bruise. An old pattern. The quiet lie she had lived too long: that she had to prove herself worthy before anyone would choose to stay. That some hearts had impenetrable walls.

But maybe… maybe it was never about fighting to be loved. And if Zayad could not meet her there—if he chose sovereignty over surrender, control over connection—then she would still rise.

Still shine.

Because stars did not need permission to be loved. They did not beg for belonging. They did not pray to be chosen.

They simply were.

She touched the leather band on her wrist—the one he'd given her, the one that still pulsed like a memory—and inhaled.

"I will not make myself small to fit inside someone else's silence," she whispered. "Not again."

CHAPTER NINE

Celeste stood barefoot on the rooftop of her private observatory, a shawl wrapped around her shoulders, her hair unbound and rippling in the desert wind. The city below was quiet, tucked into itself, but the sky —the sky was speaking.

Aldebaran had risen in its full orange glory, its light warm and unwavering. The Alpha star of Taurus. The Eye of the Bull.

Tonight, Earth was aligning with it.

And in the ancient rhythm of stars and soul, something within her was aligning too. She pressed her palm against her chest, breathing deep.

The poets say that men are made for glory...

But what of women?

She had spent her life orbiting brilliance, even her own, while staying out of reach—safe, distant, contained. But loving Zayad was none of those things. It was not glory. It was devotion. Risk. Revelation.

She had fallen in love with him the moment he had seen her, truly seen her, wrapped up in wonder. Their kiss beneath the stars had sealed it, even if she tried to deny it. Her mind with its persistent refusal was no match for her heart with its fierce certainty.

Aldebaran's light flickered across the sand dunes beyond the walls, bathing the horizon in copper fire. It was said this star was the Guardian of the Eastern Sky, the Star of Enlightenment, the Eye of Revelation, the home of guardian angels.

Celeste had once read that from the etheric sphere of Earth, a bridge stretched to Aldebaran—woven from light, through which souls could reconnect with their highest divine intention.

She closed her eyes and whispered:

"If I'm meant to walk away, give me the strength. If I'm meant to stay, give him the courage to love me without walls."

No sign appeared. No wind change. No celestial flash.

Just stillness.

And the quiet weight of truth.

She opened her journal, and began to compose what felt like a goodbye—not only to Zayad, but to the part of her that stayed small to avoid pain.

If he cannot meet me under the stars,
I will no longer wait for him in the shadows.
I have stood inside firelight and revelation.
I have seen myself clearly.
I will not dim that knowing just because he fears the light.

She paused, the ink still wet.

Tonight, Aldebaran aligns with Earth.
The gateway opens.
This is a turning point. For the world. For me.

She felt it in her bones. The shift. The invitation.

A portal of becoming.

The star overhead pulsed with warm orange fire, the kind that didn't blind, but revealed.

She gathered her things in silence. Folded the shawl. Picked up the band he had given her—the sky map once worn by his mother.

She didn't put it on.

She placed it gently in the center of the mat, beneath the open sky. A gift returned. Not in anger. But in clarity.

If he is ready to walk through this gateway with me, he will find me.

If not, I will still rise with the sun.

She descended the stairs quietly.

Behind her, Aldebaran burned.

And from the hidden realm of angels and stars, she felt a presence walk beside her—not Zayad. But the part of herself she had nearly abandoned. The one who remembered how to choose her own light.

CHAPTER TEN

He should have been in the palace.

He should have been in the meeting with the Emir of Al-Farid.

He should have been anywhere but here—standing in the courtyard, head tilted skyward, as the copper flame of Aldebaran rose higher above the minarets.

But Zayad was no longer listening to what he should do.

The light of the Eye of the Bull poured down like revelation.

The Star of Enlightenment.

The Eye of Revelation.

A fixed fire in the firmament that had guided prophets, kings, and fools alike.

And now, him.

He had spent days pretending not to feel the change. Avoiding her gaze. Shrinking from the truth of what her love might mean. Because love had always come wrapped in grief for him. It had taken before it gave. And he feared it would take her too.

But when he entered the old tower that evening and found

her shawl gone, her mat empty, and the sky map—the one his mother once pressed against her heart—left behind…

Something inside him cracked. She had not walked away in anger. She had walked away in truth. And for the first time, he was not afraid of her leaving. He was afraid she would never let him follow.

He left everything—his phone, his guards, his rank, and took just a keffiyeh, a waterskin, and his horse, Tala. He rode west, toward the sacred dunes. Toward where he knew he would find her.

The stars wheeled above him as the wind picked up, warm and whispering, as if the earth itself knew what this night meant. With each gallop, he thought of her.

Her eyes lit with starlight.

Her voice steady with ache.

The moment he had seen the words etched with silent longing in her eyes, 'Then fall.'

And how he had not.

But now—he would.

Because Aldebaran was not just a star. It was a bridge. A heavenly current pulling him toward the only truth that ever made sense. He was not meant to conquer her. He was meant to love her. To fight for their love.

And he would declare his love for her now—before the alignment passed, before the window closed, before she turned from him forever and disappeared into the starlit vastness of her own becoming.

He crested the final dune as the hour reached its peak. There—at the edge of the desert, under the sacred sky—she stood just as he knew she would.

Alone. Radiant. Unmoving. As if she had heard him coming before the wind did.

Zayad dismounted, breath caught somewhere between his

ribs and his heart. He walked the last steps. And when she turned to face him, he dropped to his knees.

Not in surrender.

But in reverence.

"I was wrong," he said, voice hoarse. "To think I had to protect myself from your love."

She didn't speak. She waited.

He reached into his tunic and pulled out the sky map—the very one she had left behind. "You don't need this to find your way," he said. "But I do. I am the one who is lost. Was lost," He corrected. "Before you"

Aldebaran pulsed above them—burning, blessing, watching.

He rose slowly, not touching her yet. "I don't want to rule over stars," he whispered. "I want to rise beside them."

He reached his hands toward hers. And the moment their palms met, the desert exhaled.

And above them, the Eye of the Bull cast its light—

Not upon rulers or rebels, but upon two souls who had finally chosen love as their path, not their prize.

CHAPTER ELEVEN

He kissed her beneath Aldebaran. Not with hunger. Not with conquest. But like a man who had crossed lifetimes to arrive in a single breath of starlight.

His hands cradled her face as if she were made of something ancient and holy.

And maybe she was.

The desert wrapped around them, wind whispering through the dunes, stardust catching in her hair. Above them, the Eye of the Bull pulsed once more—one long, knowing blink—before beginning its slow descent into the western sky.

Celeste melted into him, fingers curled into the folds of his robe, her heartbeat echoing with the truth of every whispered fear, every resisted longing.

He had come.

Not to save her.

But to stand with her.

And that, she knew, was what made the kiss sacred. When they parted, breathless and undone, she didn't speak. She simply pressed her forehead to his and closed her eyes, letting the silence say everything words could not.

Later, they lay side by side beneath the curve of a dune, the last stars fading into the pale silk of dawn. Their fingers remained entwined. No more pretending. No more distance. Just skin, warmth, and breath shared in rhythm with the rising sun.

The fire had died to embers. The night had spent itself in prophecy.

And still, she did not want to move.

He turned to her, brushing his thumb gently along the inside of her wrist where her pulse whispered the language of trust.

"Do you know what this means?" he asked softly.

She nodded, eyes still on the sky. "Everything."

He smiled, rare and unguarded. "We crossed the bridge."

She looked at him then, face bare in the morning light. "Aldebaran opened the gateway. But we had to choose to walk across."

They watched the sunrise together, wrapped in a silence that was no longer defensive, but devotional.

The light came slowly—first pale, then rose-gold, then honeyed warmth that spilled across the sand like blessing.

He kissed her fingers. She pressed her cheek to his shoulder. And the desert bore witness. There were no vows. No declarations. Only presence.

And that was everything. For now, they were no longer orbiting separate truths. They had found their alignment.

Not because the stars had demanded it.

But because, finally, they had chosen it.

Together.

CHAPTER TWELVE

The sun had fully risen by the time they reached the oasis the following morning.

It was nestled within a crescent of stone and dune, hidden from the world by walls of golden rock and the hush of wind-shaped time. Zayad had known of its existence since childhood—an ancestral place of solitude once reserved for fasting, prayer, and the washing away of burdens too great for speech.

But he had never brought anyone here. Until now.

Celeste stood at the edge of the pool, her feet bare in the sand, her linen robes loose against her skin. The water shimmered clear and still, fed by a spring that sang softly beneath the surface. Palm fronds danced overhead, catching light in emerald filaments.

She knelt and touched the water with reverence.

"It's warm," she whispered, surprised.

He nodded. "It's fed from beneath the earth. Constant. Quiet. It's said to hold the memory of every soul who ever wept here."

Celeste looked up at him. "And what do you bring here?"

"My silence," he said. "And now—my heart."

He turned, giving her space. Not because he feared her body, but because he honored her spirit.

She stepped into the water slowly, as if entering a temple.

It embraced her, lapping against her thighs, her waist, her ribs. She let herself sink beneath the surface, eyes closed, arms outstretched like wings. And for a moment, she felt everything fall away—fear, grief, old betrayals.

She surfaced with a gasp, water dripping from her hair, her lashes, her collarbones like molten silver. She smiled— freely, fiercely.

He watched from the shore, barefoot, cloaked in stillness.

"Come," she said softly, and he did.

He stepped into the water with her, and when he reached her, they stood face to face in the shallows, breath mingling.

She cupped his face in her hands, her touch featherlight.

"I want to begin again," she said.

He lowered his forehead to hers, eyes closed. "Then let this be our baptism."

Together, they submerged once more—two sovereign souls washed in light.

When they emerged, they did not speak. They dressed slowly beneath the palms, letting the sun dry their skin. She fastened the sky map band back onto her wrist. He traced its edge with his thumb.

No longer a relic. Now, a vow.

They sat beneath a tamarisk tree, sharing figs and silence, wrapped in a peace that didn't need proving.

The world still waited. So did duty, and legacy, and shadows.

But not yet.

For now, the oasis held them.

And the water remembered.

CHAPTER THIRTEEN

The gates closed behind them as they returned to Qamar with a sound like finality.

Not thunderous, not loud. Just a low, ancient groan of iron and stone that echoed in Celeste's spine.

She sat beside Zayad in the open-roofed transport, the city rising around them like a mirage made of gold and scrutiny. Minarets shimmered. Courtyards bloomed. But behind every silk-draped window and carved archway, she could feel it—

Eyes. Watching. Weighing. Whispering.

They had crossed the desert as equals. Souls in starlight.

But here, in the capital, the old hierarchies snapped back into place like unseen chains.

A ripple had already begun.

The prince returned with a woman. A foreigner. An academic. A commoner.

She heard it in the way the guards bowed lower to Zayad than to her.

Felt it in the delay before the steward opened her side of **the carriage**.

Saw it in the flicker of narrowed eyes from the court

advisor who had once praised her research—before it belonged to her.

By the time they entered the palace, the air itself had thickened with rumor.

That evening, Zayad was summoned to an emergency council session.

Celeste wasn't invited.

She wandered alone through the amber-lit halls, ancient stars carved into the walls, arches shaped like crescent moons. The palace was beautiful. But beauty, she was learning, could also be a mask.

Later, when she found a quiet corner of the royal library, an old servant passed by and left a folded scrap of parchment on the table without meeting her eye.

She is not one of us.
She is dust beneath his name.

Celeste sat back slowly, the insult cold against her skin. She had studied quantum mechanics. Mapped stars no one else could see. She had loved quietly, with her whole soul, and had asked for nothing but honesty in return.

And yet—here, she was reduced to dust. Her education, so fiercely attained, was weaponized against her.

Later that night, Zayad returned.

His jaw was tight. His steps heavy.

He didn't speak as he entered her chamber. But his eyes—burning with fury—told her everything.

"They questioned your presence," he said. "Your bloodline. Your 'right' to walk beside me."

Celeste stood still, spine straight. "And what did you say?"

Zayad met her gaze. "That I walk beside no one I do not bow to in spirit."

Silence. Then:

"And what did they say?"

He stepped toward her. "That I've lost my mind. That I've been bewitched. Seduced by the stars."

She smiled, though it ached. "Maybe you have."

He cupped her face. "Then I will build a kingdom on that madness."

But even as he kissed her forehead, she felt the storm gathering.

The old world would not surrender easily.

Not to love without rules

Not to stars without boundaries.

And certainly not to a woman with intelligence in her veins, dust on her feet and light in her eyes.

CHAPTER FOURTEEN

The morning sun spilled gold across the marble floors of the audience hall, but the warmth did not reach the corners where power plotted in shadows.

Celeste stood beside Zayad on the raised dais, her linen robes plain against the opulence surrounding her. The grand vizier's voice rang out across the chamber, reading from a rolled parchment sealed in crimson wax.

"In light of recent disruptions to the delicate balance of the House of Al-Rami, and in the interest of national stability and royal lineage, it is hereby advised that the prince's association with Dr. Celeste Valente be paused pending a formal investigation into her influence, origin, and intentions."

Paused.

Pending investigation.

Celeste felt the words like a blade dressed in velvet.

Zayad's fingers twitched at his side, but he remained silent, his face carved from stone.

She did not speak either.

Because to do so would be to dignify the charade.

The vizier continued, listing fabricated concerns—her

status as a foreigner, the threat of academic influence on national affairs, the "unprecedented impropriety" of a royal consort lacking noble blood.

By the time the decree was finished, Celeste felt no anger. Only clarity.

This was not about her.

This was about the fear of the old world being dismantled by something it could not control: an educated woman unafraid of stars, sand, or silence.

Later that day, she was escorted to the east wing—for her comfort and protection, they claimed. A gilded exile. Soft seclusion.

The hall was beautiful. Arched windows overlooking the rose gardens. Mosaics of constellations tiled into the floor. But she recognized the move for what it was: containment.

Zayad had tried to refuse the separation. She had touched his cheek before they were parted and whispered, "Let them think they've succeeded. The stars are not moved by doors."

Still, alone in her rooms, she allowed herself to grieve.

But not for long.

Because that night, something unexpected happened.

A knock at her door.

It creaked open to reveal an older woman in a faded emerald robe, her eyes ringed with kohl, her hands ink-stained. Celeste recognized her—Layla bint Haran, the court's forgotten astronomer. Once the star-reader to Zayad's mother. Now little more than a relic in the archives.

That night, they spread star charts across the tiled floor.

Traced Aldebaran's path with whispered reverence.

Spoke of things the court had long forgotten—wisdom, purpose, light.

Celeste smiled for the first time in days. The walls were not closing in.

They were echoing. And in the quiet spaces between the old world's fear, she was building something unshakable:

A constellation of quiet power.

CHAPTER FIFTEEN

That night, when the knock came, Celeste expected a servant. Instead, the door opened to four women. Each bearing something the court had underestimated—memory, magic, and vision.

The first was Layla bint Haran, the court's former astronomer. She stepped inside with quiet authority, a scroll tucked under her arm.

Behind her came two more—Samira, a scribe whose hands bore ink from copying forbidden histories, and Raisa, a desert healer with lapis rings and the scent of rosemary on her skin.

And then, last, stepping over the threshold with eyes like stormlight, came Imani.

Celeste felt her presence before she spoke—a stillness that wasn't absence but depth. Her garments were deep indigo, embroidered with star symbols. A veil draped her silver hair. She carried nothing but a small wooden box and a candle.

"I am the daughter of prophets," Imani said softly. "And the stars have waited for you."

Celeste blinked. "Waited?"

Imani nodded. "You were born under a rare sky. I've seen it only once—when Aldebaran rose in exact conjunction with the sun in the eastern sky, casting its orange fire over the horizon like a second dawn."

She unrolled a worn chart. "You said you were born in Florence, yes? Just before sunrise?"

Celeste nodded, stunned. "Yes."

Imani's fingers moved across the parchment with reverence, whispering old names of planets and stars like prayers.

"Aldebaran," she said, pointing to a glowing intersection on the chart, "was rising on your Ascendant. That means it is not only your guiding star—it is your face to the world. The Eye of the Bull. The Guardian of the East. The Bridge between Earth and the Divine."

Layla gasped. "That alignment comes only once in centuries."

Imani looked up, her voice slow and sure.

"You are not here by accident, Celeste. You are the eye through which truth is revealed. You have come to awaken the royal house—not to destroy it, but to restore its vision."

Celeste sat down slowly on the mosaic floor, her heart thudding in her chest.

She had spent a lifetime among observatories and equations. She had loved the stars as light, as math, as constant. But tonight, she saw them as something else entirely— witnesses. Messengers. Mirrors.

"What am I supposed to do?" she whispered.

Imani smiled gently.

"Be who you are. The stars will do the rest."

CHAPTER SIXTEEN

Two days later, Zayad entered the Royal Council Chamber before the others arrived. He stood alone for a moment, staring out the narrow window carved high in the eastern wall. The morning sun was rising, pouring molten light across the sandstone floors. Aldebaran's fire had faded from the night sky, but its influence lingered.

He could still feel her hand in his.

Still hear her voice saying, "Let them think they've succeeded. The stars are not moved by doors."

He had left her in the East Wing, not out of defeat, but by design.

Let the court believe they had won a concession. Let the traditionalists think they had backed him into a corner. Let the patriarchs whisper behind draped curtains.

He was not retreating. He was coiling. Ready to strike.

The chamber doors opened. The council filed in, robed and perfumed, eyes sharp. Grand Vizier Al-Rashid took his place at the table with a smirk barely hidden behind formal courtesy.

"The matter of Dr. Valente's continued presence—" the vizier began.

Zayad raised his hand. "Is not up for discussion."

The room stilled.

"Your Highness," Al-Rashid said carefully, "there are protocols. The people—"

"—have not been consulted," Zayad interrupted, his voice calm, lethal. "I intend to change that."

He pulled a scroll from his sleeve and placed it on the table.

"A public symposium," he said. "In one week. On celestial knowledge and its integration into governance. I will be hosting it. Dr. Valente will be speaking."

Shock rippled through the room.

"Impossible," one of the old lords spat. "She is not of Qamari blood."

Zayad's expression didn't change. "No. But her knowledge runs deeper than most dynasties."

Another voice: "You would place a foreign woman on the podium of power?"

Zayad leaned forward, eyes cold. "I would place a truth-teller where the truth belongs."

He let the silence sharpen around them.

Then, more softly, he added, "You forget—I am not my father."

At that, even Al-Rashid fell quiet.

Later, in the privacy of his study, Zayad summoned his most trusted aide, Malik.

"Begin inquiries," he said. "Gather every record of royal consorts from outside noble bloodlines. Find precedent. Find contradiction. Bring me history the council cannot twist."

Malik bowed. "And the symposium?"

"Open to the public," Zayad said. "No controlled guest list. Let the people hear her. Let them see the fire for themselves."

As Malik left, Zayad sat back in his chair, exhaling slowly. He was not fighting for Celeste out of sentiment. He was defending a future she had helped him see. One ruled not by lineage, but vision.

And if the council wanted war, he would give them something far more dangerous:

A woman who had aligned herself with the stars.

CHAPTER SEVENTEEN

Celeste sat cross-legged on the tiled floor of the East Wing library, scrolls and ink bottles scattered around her like offerings. Moonlight poured through the carved windows, pooling on the mosaic of the heavens beneath her feet.

It was three days before the Symposium and she had written nothing.

Not a single word.

Despite years of research and study, all her lectures and fieldwork and quietly blistering essays and academic papers published in scientific journals, she felt unprepared. This was different. This wasn't about theory. This was about standing in the fire of a kingdom and shining without apology.

The women moved softly around her—Samira organizing notes, Raisa brewing a tea of blue lotus and cardamom, Layla cross-referencing ancient speeches from women philosophers of Qamar's past.

And then Imani entered. As always, she carried no books, no papers—only presence.

"You are trying to write with your mind," she said gently. "But this speech must come from your soul."

Celeste exhaled, pinching the bridge of her nose. "I don't know where to begin."

Imani reached for her small wooden box and retrieved a folded chart—the natal sky they had read together days before. "Aldebaran is in your third house," she said, laying it before her. "This is your place of voice. Of speaking. Of writing."

Celeste looked at the brilliant orange mark over the house of communication.

"A sword of light," Imani continued. "You were born to speak what others fear to name. To cut through illusion with words that wound and heal in the same breath."

Celeste glanced down at her hands. "Then why does it hurt to speak in front of so much opposition?"

Imani's gaze softened. "Because your Moon is in Pisces, square to that sword. You feel everything. Empathy softens your truth. Sometimes it binds it. You sense injustice like a bruise under your ribs, but voicing it… it feels like betrayal."

Celeste nodded, her voice nearly a whisper. "Yes, sometimes the more peaceful solution is to remain silent. To avoid harm I never intended."

"That is the conflict you feel so deeply, because of who you are. But this tension," Imani said, her finger tracing the line of her natal chart, "is your power. You don't speak to dominate. You speak to reveal. And Aldebaran opposing your Sun in Libra—this is the sacred mirror. You came to embody peace, yes—but not by pleasing everyone. That is impossible. By speaking moral clarity, even when it breaks the harmony."

Celeste swallowed hard. The words settled in her chest like an anchor of light.

Imani's voice dropped to a hush.

"You are not here to avoid conflict. You are here to illuminate it with truth. You are not responsible for how the truth is received, only for delivering it."

The room stilled. Even the candle flames seemed to listen.

Samira stepped forward then, holding a scroll. "You wrote this once, years ago," she said, her voice trembling. "A line in the margin of a thesis. I copied it."

She read aloud:

"Justice is not the absence of chaos. It is the courage to speak when silence becomes complicity."

Celeste stared at her, startled. She had forgotten she ever wrote that.

"It sounds like a beginning," Layla said.

Celeste slowly lowered herself to the floor, drew the scroll close, and dipped her pen into ink.

Not with fear. With flame.

Over the next three days, the library transformed into a sanctuary of becoming. The women moved like constellations around her—offering phrases, memories, poems, rhythms. Celeste wrote late into the night, pausing only to drink, to cry, to breathe.

She spoke aloud to the stars. To Aldebaran.

"Help me become what I already am."

By the time dawn arrived on the day of the symposium, she had written something more than a speech. She had written a reckoning.

And when she rose, draped in soft desert linen, with a

constellation pendant resting above her heart and the sky map once again tied at her wrist—

She no longer wondered if she belonged.

She remembered that the stars had never needed permission to rise.

CHAPTER EIGHTEEN

The high-arched ceilings of the Grand Hall of Qamar glittered with gold-inlaid constellations as the crowds gathered beneath it. Never had so many people come in search of answers.

Incense curled around them like prayer around the edges of marble columns. Nobles in silks and diplomats in dark robes lined the front. Behind them, scholars, students, traders —men and women from across the kingdom—gathered in a rustling sea of anticipation.

The air thrummed with curiosity, tension, and something else: fate.

Zayad sat at the center of the *dais*, robed in deep midnight blue, the Al-Rami crest at his shoulder. He looked calm. But his fingers tapped a steady rhythm against the carved arm of his chair. Only Malik, standing behind him, noticed the slight tremor in his jaw.

Then the doors opened. And Celeste entered.

She crossed the threshold with a stillness so absolute it was as if she was born for this moment. She radiated soverignity, silencing the room more effectively than any trumpet or decree.

She wore no crown. No jewels. Just ivory linen cinched at the waist, her shoulders bare, her hair braided simply down her back. At her wrist, the sky map shimmered.

Behind her walked Layla, Samira, Raisa, and Imani. They took their place at the side of the chamber like priestesses of a forgotten order.

Celeste moved to the podium of carved cedar and silver. She placed her scroll on it, ran her fingers once across its edge, then looked up. Her eyes swept the hall—not with fear, but with fire.

She did not bow. She did not wait for permission to speak. She did not lower her gaze to read her notes.

She began from her heart.

"When I was a child, I was taught that stars were distant. Cold. Scientific. The keeper of secrets. When I became a woman, I discovered they were something else entirely— truth, burning."

A rustle moved through the chamber.

"I was not born in Qamar. My ancestors held no titles. I carry no noble blood. But I carry something older. I carry the light."

She waited for the audible gasps of shock to settle. She watched as the astrologers in the crowd straightened in stern resolution. She smiled as the court priest shifted to the back of the hall.

"In my chart," she continued, "Aldebaran rises in my third house—the house of words, of voice. Of truth-telling."

"And I carry a voice aligned with Aldebaran—the Eye of Revelation." She paused and looked to Imani, drawing strength from her nod of encouragement. "It sits square to my moon in Pisces—so I feel deeply. *Sometimes too deeply*. And that depth has made me hesitate, has made me silent. But since coming to your kingdom I have learned that silence, in the face of injustice, becomes a betrayal. And so I must speak. The stars command it."

A hush fell so complete, even the torches seemed to flicker more softly.

"I speak not to seek power, but to reveal where power has grown blind. I speak not for revenge, but for remembrance of what this kingdom once was. A place where wisdom mattered more than lineage. Where the stars were read as guidance, not threat. Where their light was born of Spirit not sorcery."

She took a breath, gathering strength as her voice dropped into deeper truths. "I do not come to rule. I come to serve the light. And if that light is too bright—it is because it is beginning to reach the shadows."

She looked out over the crowd. Some bowed their heads. Others stared, unblinking. A few, the ones she'd expected, burned with quiet fury.

But she saw others… leaning forward. Listening. "Let the old world judge me by my country of birth, my blood, my gender. But let the new world remember me for my voice. For I speak not as royalty—but as a woman who refuses to kneel when the stars call her to rise."

She stepped back.

And the room… remained suspended in stunned silence. No clapping. No gasps. Just the hum of something ancient realigning.

Zayad stood slowly.

And for the first time in royal history, the prince bowed to her, a commoner.

Not in platitude. But in reverence.

CHAPTER NINETEEN

The council chambers fractured just before nightfall. Some stormed out in protest, their robes snapping behind them like wounded pride. Others remained, silent and unmoving, processing what had been said beneath the torchlight of truth.

One minister whispered, "It was heresy."

Another murmured, "It was prophecy."

And outside, in the courtyard where olive trees bloomed and the sky map was carved into the stone, the people of Qamar gathered.

They didn't riot. They didn't kneel.

They talked.

Not just of her words, but of her presence. Of how she had stood—not as a queen, not as a foreigner—but as if the stars themselves had placed her feet there.

For the first time in years, the people were watching their leaders, not for approval, but for integrity.

And the council felt it.

. . .

Inside the palace, Zayad stood before the great window in his private study, his hands braced against the sill. Outside, the sky had begun to darken again. Aldebaran no longer blazed, but he felt its echo in his ribs.

Celeste entered without knocking.

He turned. The look they exchanged was not relief. It was something deeper—an acknowledgment of what they had both risked and become.

She stepped toward him, the soft rustle of her robes the only sound between them. "Did I fracture the kingdom?" she asked, half a breath.

Zayad shook his head. "No. You fractured the lie it was built on."

She reached for his hand. He took it without hesitating. They stood hand-in-hand facing the evening sky—two souls forged in clarity.

"I thought I would feel afraid," she whispered. "But I don't."

"That's because you spoke from the place they cannot touch."

He drew her closer. "You were never just a guest in this land," he said. "You were always a flame meant to light what we'd forgotten."

She laid her head on his chest, listening to the beat of his heart. He kissed the crown of her head. And in that moment, it no longer mattered whether the court accepted her. Because the stars already had.

Zayad drew back just enough to see her face, his eyes searching hers—not for permission, but for promise.

"Celeste…"

She looked up, breath caught.

"I was born into duty. Trained to wield power like a sword. But you—" he paused, voice thick with emotion—

"you taught me to speak with fire, not fear. You showed me that true strength lives in vulnerability. In truth. In love."

He reached into the folds of his robe. And this time, it wasn't a relic or a map.

It was a ring.

Not just any ring—a work of celestial art.

"A band of luminous star-metal from the sacred mines of Qamar, set with a rare opal," he murmured as her gaze bounced from the ring to his eyes."

The light in her eyes shimmered like the galaxy forged in stone, like the giant rocks on the ring of promise cuhioned in silg. Around the opal, huge diamonds traced the constellation they had watched rise together in the desert sky.

"I had it made for the one who turned my world from shadow to starlight," he said softly, reverently.

He dropped to one knee, the starlit courtyard holding its breath.

"Marry me, Celeste. Not because it's expected. Not because it's tradition. But because we've seen each other in the dark and chosen to stay."

He held out the ring.

"No crown could shine brighter than the light you've given me."

And in the hush between heartbeats, he was not a prince, not a ruler, but a man—offering not power, but partnership.

The stars burned above them.

"Your move, Celeste."

Celeste froze.

Not from fear.

But from the tremble of something breaking open.

She had dreamed of this once. Before disappointment

taught her to shrink. Before betrayal convinced her that grand gestures were traps and promises were just prettier lies.

But this...

This wasn't illusion. This was truth. Raw, radiant, terrifying in its tenderness.

And suddenly, she wasn't the girl who dimmed her light to be loved. She was the woman who had stood before the Council and burned with her truth.

The ache in her chest softened. Not vanished—transformed. No longer the ache of being unseen. But the ache of being seen... and still chosen.

Her eyes shimmered. She stepped forward, not out of obligation, but out of sovereignty. She whispered, "I spent so long waiting for someone to choose me... and now I see— this is me choosing, too."

She offered him her hand. "Yes," she said, steady and sure. "I will marry you. "Yes. A thousand times yes."

As he slipped the ring onto her finger, it flared with light —like the universe had just said Amen.

And one star, somewhere, fell.

CHAPTER TWENTY

Three nights.

That's all it took.

Three nights after Zayad's proposal beneath the blazing stars, Celeste became his wife.

Not because she was rushed. Not because it was expected. But because the number three meant something to both of them now.

Three stars make Orion's Belt—the guidepost of every stargazer.

Three phases mark the moon—waxing, full, and waning —each carrying its own power.

And three nights had passed since her world had tilted into orbit with his.

Zayad, ever a man of conviction and command, had spoken just once to the council: "The stars have aligned. I will not wait."

And no one dared to argue.

Now, under a sky unmarred by doubt, the dunes stood witness to a union written long before the world was named.

A private pavilion of white silk had been raised in the

open desert. Candles flickered in carved lanterns. Wild jasmine clung to the air. No throne, no audience, no politics—just two souls and the universe that had conspired to bring them back to each other.

Celeste stood barefoot in the sand, her gown soft as a sigh, woven with threads of silver that shimmered like the Milky Way. Around her wrist, the leather band he'd given her remained—a constant, quiet vow. But on her finger now glowed a ring forged with fire-opal and stardust, set in ancient gold—dazzling, defiant, and destined.

Zayad waited at the altar, a carved stone slab kissed by centuries of sun. His robe was deep midnight, his crown absent, his hands steady. But it was his eyes—storm-dark, sure—that anchored her.

She reached him, and he whispered, "Three nights ago, I gave you my truth. Tonight, I give you everything."

Celeste blinked back tears, but didn't look away. "Three nights ago, I remembered who I was. Tonight, I choose who I become—with you."

No priest. No pomp.

Just vows spoken in the language of stars.

"I will not ask you to kneel," he said softly. "But I will ask you to rise with me. As partner. As flame. As the voice the world has waited for."

She took his hand, and together, they laid their palms on the ancient stone, where once the ancestors had traced maps in the sky.

A breeze stirred the veil of her hair. Overhead, Aldebaran pulsed with radiant clarity—watching, blessing, remembering.

And when he kissed her—finally, fully, as his queen—the sky above them opened like a page turning.

The third kiss of the night. The one that sealed it.

Later, in the sacred quiet of their wedding tent, he undid the clasps of her gown with reverence, as though unwrapping a constellation. She ran her hands over his chest, mapping the story of a man who had once feared love might ruin him—but who had chosen it anyway.

They didn't speak of fear. They didn't speak of fate.

Only love.

Only light.

And as they lay together beneath the open dome of stars, the third night after the vow, Aldebaran still burned above them.

Just like the love that no longer hid.

Just like the woman who no longer dimmed.

Just like the king who had finally fallen—and risen—in the name of something far more powerful than sovereignty.

CHAPTER TWENTY-ONE

C hange did not thunder. It moved like water.

In the markets, a week later, young women quoted Celeste's words between loaves of bread and bolts of dyed linen. In the libraries, scholars dug out lost manuscripts by Qamari women—mathematicians, mystics, astronomers erased by time and titles.

In tea houses, poets debated whether Aldebaran had risen that night just a fraction brighter. In the temples, astrologers argued. Some called it heresy—aligning personal identity with fixed stars, treating a foreigner's birth chart as prophecy.

Others, especially the younger generation, whispered that perhaps the old interpretations had grown too narrow. That maybe, just maybe, the stars had chosen Celeste because the people had forgotten how to listen.

And in the palace?

The council was still reeling. Half insisted Zayad had been bewitched. That he'd lost sight of royal duty. The other half—quieter, sharper—were beginning to realize something else.

The people were listening to her.

Not in worship. Not in fear.

In recognition.

That night, Celeste and Zayad sat in the high garden at the edge of the palace walls, the city below a mosaic of lanterns and whispers.

They sat beneath a fig tree, side by side on a stone bench. No guards. No courtiers. Just desert air and the scent of jasmine curling through the night.

"I never imagined this," she said softly.

Zayad turned to her. "What?"

"That truth could travel this far. That words spoken in stillness could move stone."

He was silent for a moment. Then: "What would you build, if they stopped trying to tear it down?"

She smiled. "A school. For girls. For women who've been told they're too much or too little."

He nodded. "And if I no longer wore a crown?"

She turned to him, eyes glinting. "Then you'd wear something better. Vision."

He took her hand. "I don't want to rule in the way they taught me. I want to rebuild something with you. Not for power. For meaning."

Celeste leaned into him, her head resting on his shoulder.

"Then let's begin," she whispered.

"Now?" he asked, smiling.

"No. Soon. After the stars shift again."

They looked up together.

Aldebaran had dipped below the horizon, but its echo remained—a quiet blaze carried in their bones.

The light was no longer only above them. It was between them. Within them. And somewhere, in the hushed corners of the kingdom, a new story was already taking root.

CHAPTER TWENTY-TWO

Q*amar – Moon of First Planting*
The school opened with no banners.
No parade.
No royal decree.

Only an open courtyard, sunlight on stone, and the scent of wild orange blossoms from the nearby grove.

They called it *Bayt al-Nujūm*—The House of Stars.

It began with twelve students.

Some were daughters of tradesmen. Some, former scribes. One was the granddaughter of a servant who had learned to read by moonlight using scraps of discarded scrolls. All had one thing in common: they had been told no—too many times, too many ways.

Celeste stood at the entrance that first morning, a linen-bound notebook in her arms, her heart pounding not with fear but with fierce devotion. Zayad stood beside her in plain robes, his hands behind his back, his presence quiet and unwavering.

Imani had come, too. She wore indigo once more and

whispered blessings in the old tongue as each student passed through the carved archway.

And behind the gates?

Resistance.

A small crowd had gathered—critics, traditionalists, self-appointed guardians of legacy. They carried nothing but words, yet they hurled them with precision.

"This is not our way."

"She's poisoning our women."

"Knowledge should not be handed to everyone like bread."

Celeste heard them all.

But she didn't flinch.

She turned, not toward the critics, but toward her students. She opened her notebook. Read the first line of the first lesson:

"The stars are for everyone.

Just because they were kept from you doesn't mean they were never yours."

And then—the ripple.

It began with one man from the crowd stepping forward. A spice merchant whose daughter had once brought home a sketch of the moon and been punished for dreaming.

"I will fund your next classroom," he said simply.

Gasps.

Then a court astrologer, long silent, approached. "I would like to teach astronomy. If you'll have me."

And then a veiled woman from the back—voice shaking but steady:

"My mother always said a mind is a garden. She never learned to plant it.

I want to learn."

The critics fell silent.

Because truth had multiplied.

And the people were beginning to see it grow.

That night, Zayad and Celeste walked through the school's quiet halls, tracing the stars carved into the tile, listening to the echo of lessons just beginning.

"Do you think it will last?" she asked.

He turned to her. "It already has."

They stood in the center of the courtyard, where a sundial marked time by the stars. A jasmine vine curled along the stone arch overhead, releasing its perfume into the warm night air.

"I didn't expect so much resistance," she said softly.

He reached for her hand.

"No one does when they begin to rise."

Celeste looked up—no longer searching for Aldebaran.

She had become the light she used to chase.

CHAPTER TWENTY-THREE

Bayt al-Nujūm – *Season of First Rains*

Rain came rarely in Qamar, but that morning, a soft mist clung to the olive leaves, beading on jasmine petals and pooling gently in the mosaic cracks of the courtyard. The sky was pale and hushed, as though the stars had lowered their voices for something sacred to unfold.

Celeste stood alone in the observatory tower of the school, her palms resting lightly on the stone railing. Below, the girls gathered for their morning reading, Layla's voice carrying softly across the tiled courtyard.

But Celeste could not focus on the words. Because her body—so familiar to her—was whispering in an entirely new language. It had started as a hush. A sense of heaviness, yes, but not of burden—of presence.

The kind of quiet you feel just before a revelation.

She had charted stars. Measured orbits. Tracked lunar drift. But this—this was not data. It was life. A new constellation stirring beneath her skin.

Behind her, the door creaked open. Zayad entered without a word, sensing the gravity in the room.

She turned to him, the softest smile breaking across her face. One hand rose to her belly—not yet visible, but known. "We're not alone anymore," she whispered.

Zayad's smile shone like a thousand stars, illuminating the room with his joy. "Are you certain, *habiti*?" he asked as he stepped closer.

She nodded. "Beyond doubt."

He reached out, his palm meeting hers where life had already begun to gather.

They stood together in sacred silence, touching the child awakening in her womb..

After a long breath, Celeste looked up at Zayad. "A new star appeared last night. Just beyond the shoulder of Taurus. I saw it while you slept."

Zayad's voice was reverent. "What do they call it?"

"I don't know yet," she said. "But it feels like a miracle. I think it belongs to our child."

"A child born of light," he murmured. "Just like her mother."

"What makes you so sure it will be a girl?"

"I'm not. It's a feeling."

"A feeling," she laughed. "Will you be disappointed?"

"Disappointed. Why would I be disappointed?"

"That your firstborn, your heir, is not a son."

"You tease me, my love. You know I have already amended the rules of succession. Boy or girl, it makes no difference. But that is one thing on which I will not bend."

"And that is?"

"We will raise a child who knows the sound of truth, the shape of stars, and the scent of jasmine after rain."

She touched his hair, her fingers curling gently. "And I will teach our children that they are born not from power, but from purpose."

Above them, the clouds parted. A shaft of sunlight fell across the tower stones like a blessing.

And somewhere in the east, a new star continued to rise, orbiting north.

CHAPTER TWENTY-FOUR

Qamar – Nine Months Later

The child was born just before dawn.

The sky above the palace glowed with the gentle fire of a triple alignment: Venus, Aldebaran, and the Moon, braided like a celestial crown across the eastern horizon.

Midwives moved softly around the birthing chamber. Jasmine oil burned in quiet reverence. A prayer bowl chimed once, then stilled. And in the hush between night and morning, a new voice entered the world.

Celeste held her daughter to her chest, tears falling silently into the child's dark, silken hair. Zayad knelt beside them, his forehead pressed to both their hands. He said nothing. There were no words holy enough for this.

The child opened her eyes, dark blue like the midnight sky, wide and unblinking, like she was already remembering the stars.

They named her Noor.

Light.

. . .

By the time Noor could walk barefoot through the olive grove behind the school, Bayt al-Nujūm had grown from a court-yard of twelve students to a sprawling sanctuary of learning, truth, and quiet transformation.

New classrooms had been added—open-air amphitheaters and vaulted libraries etched with star maps and poems by forgotten women of Qamar. A healing wing trained midwives, herbalists, and moon-cycle guides. A tower was built for celestial observation, with girls now charting skies that had once been forbidden to them.

Resistance hadn't vanished—but it had grown quieter.

Because the truth, once lived, is harder to erase.

The women who had once been called foolish, foreign, or dangerous now carried knowledge through every street of Qamar. They became teachers. Historians. Council advisors. Mothers raising children to think in constellations, not cages.

And every so often, a girl would ask Celeste, "How did all of this begin?"

And she would smile, touch the star map still knotted at her wrist, and say:"With one star, and one voice brave enough to speak beneath it."

That evening, as the lanterns were lit and the children prepared for stargazing, Celeste and Zayad stood hand in hand atop the observation tower. Noor slept against Zayad's chest, her breath warm and even.

Below them, the school pulsed with laughter, firelight, and the sound of pages turning. Above them, the stars burned steadily and near, no longer distant.

Celeste looked up at the shoulder of Taurus, where Alde-baran now shared the sky with a new, unnamed light.

And in that moment, she knew:
They had not only rewritten a kingdom.
They had rewoven the sky.

EPILOGUE

The *Temple of Light – Thirty Years Later*
Night fell like silk over the city of Qamar.
But it was no longer the same city.

Minarets now rose beside observatories. Public squares echoed not with decrees but with music, poetry, and the names of stars whispered in three languages. The House of Stars had become a university of light, its teachings now sent by letter and beacon to distant lands.

And at the center of its great stone courtyard, beneath a canopy of olive trees and softly glowing lanterns, stood Noor.

Tall. Graceful. Quietly fierce.

Her robe was woven with threads of silver, its hem embroidered with constellations. Around her wrist, she wore a narrow leather band—cracked and weathered from years of wear, still etched with gold stars.

Her mother's sky map, and before that, her paternal grandmother's.

Tonight, she would speak beneath the stars for the first time—not as a daughter, not as a student—but as the Keeper of the Observatory, a title passed not through blood, but through vision.

The Temple of Light was full.

Scholars. Farmers. Pilgrims. Women who had once been girls silenced at birth. Men who had once scoffed and now bowed their heads in reverence. Children sat cross-legged at the front, eyes wide, gazing at her like she was a comet made of memory.

Noor raised her gaze to the heavens.

A new star had appeared beside Aldebaran. It had no name yet. But she felt it was already speaking.

"Once," she began, her voice like moonlight over stone, "a woman stood alone beneath the stars and was told she didn't belong."

Noor paused, letting the silence listen. "She didn't fight to be accepted. She remembered that the stars had always accepted her. And from that remembering, a kingdom was reborn."

She placed a hand over her heart and gestured to her mother, seated beside her father, in place of honour.

"That woman was my mother. And tonight, I speak in her name—but also in my grandmother's and in mine. Because this light… was never theirs alone. It is yours now. Ours. Forever."

Above her, Aldebaran blazed. And beside it, the new star shimmered to life.

Not as a sign of arrival. But as the mark of what had already been begun. It was time for Noor to follow her own True North and find the destiny that awaited her, written in the stars.

*** THE END ***

. . .

Keep reading for an excerpt of Noor's love story, Liberated By The Sheikh, and for exclusive excerpts from other Sheikh-inspired romances by Mollie

AUTHOR'S NOTE

As a child, I was always fascinated by the stars.

I used to imagine myself flying on a magic carpet, weaving through the night sky, dipping and soaring between constellations like a traveler in a storybook. My favorite nursery rhymes—perhaps they were yours, too—included Twinkle, Twinkle, Little Star. I still remember singing, how I wonder what you are, and meaning every word with my whole heart.

That sense of awe never left me. One evening, years later, I stood outside with my godmother, gazing up at the sky. I turned to her and said, "Don't you think it's amazing that we're just suspended here, in the middle of space?" She looked at me, entirely serious, and asked, "Are you going crazy?"

That moment stayed with me—both the wonder and the loneliness of it.

And maybe that's what planted the seed for this story.

Awakened by the Sheikh is, at its heart, a love letter to awe. To women who have dared to dream beyond what they were told. To those who find solace in the stars when the earth feels unsteady. I imagined a woman—Celeste—who made a career out of loving the cosmos, because it felt safer than risking her heart with another human. A woman who could read the language of galaxies, but still struggled to trust her own longing for connection, for closeness, for love.

I wondered, as authors do: What if it felt safer to love stars than to risk loving again—especially after betrayal? What if someone, unexpected and true, saw you anyway? What if he didn't just see you... but stayed?

This love story marks the beginning of a sweeping romantic series—Desert Royals—and I'm so grateful you've chosen to begin here, beneath the stars.

If Celeste's story touches you, if you find beauty in her journey, I'd be deeply honored if you would consider leaving a review. Your words help readers discover these stories—and help authors like me keep sharing them.

With love and light,

Mollie

xxx

DID THIS STORY TOUCH YOUR HEART

If this story touched your heart, I'd love to hear from you! Please consider leaving a review on **Amazon** or **Goodreads** —your words mean more than you know and help other readers discover these stories.

📖 **Keep reading for exclusive excerpts from the next books in this and other series!**

🤍 **Leave a review on Amazon**

🤍 **Share your thoughts on Goodreads and/or Bookbub**

And don't miss other books in **The Sheikh's Untamed Brides Series!**

🔥 **Claimed by the Sheikh** (Tariq and Melanie's story)
📖 Read here!

🔥 **Stolen by the Sheikh** (Anwar and Lucy's story)
📖 Read here!

Thank you for being part of this journey—your love for romance is what keeps these stories alive.

With gratitude and love,
♡ Mollie Mathews

JOIN THE CLUB

Never miss a new release or giveaway! Sign up for Mollie's newsletter to stay in the loop—and receive a free love story. Check out a full list of books and bio at www.molliemathews.com. Follow Mollie on Social Media as @Molliewritesromance (because she does) And if you loved this book, please take a moment to leave a review once you're done. Thank you!

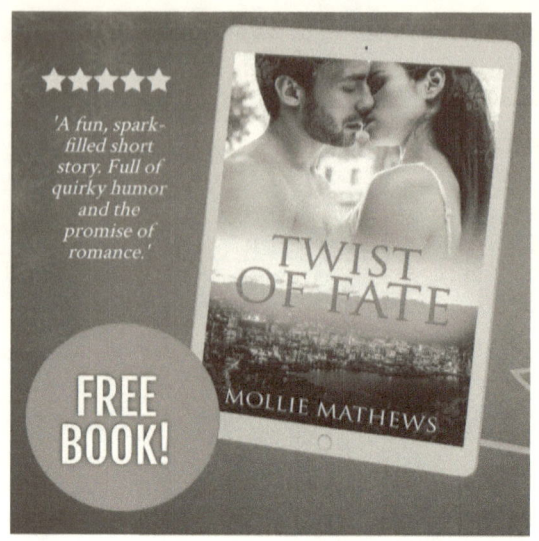

EXCERPT: LIBERATED BY THE SHEIKH

AUTHOR'S NOTE

Dear Reader,

When I imagined Noor, I saw her as a child born of vision and fire—but I also felt her weight. The daughter of two beloved figures. Raised in reverence. Expected to shine.

But what happens when a soul believes she must live up to love, instead of living from it?

That is Noor's story. A woman who does not lack love, but who believes her parents have already perfected it. Who thinks anything she creates in its shadow will be too small, too flawed, too unworthy.

And yet… the stars have something else in mind.

In the next chapter of this world, Noor will discover what her mother once did: that love is not a legacy we replicate—it is a flame we awaken in our own way.

Not to imitate.

But to liberate.

With love,

Mollie

Thank you for joining me on this journey. There are more sheikh romances to come, and I can't wait to share them with you!

With love and gratitude,

♡ Mollie Mathews

LIBERATED BY THE SHEIKH

In a kingdom of shadows, he became her shield of light.

Noor was born into love.

Daughter of a woman who spoke to the stars and a man who ruled with a soul anchored in truth, she was raised in the sanctuary of wonder, reverence, and devotion.

But what happens when a soul believes she must live up to love, instead of living from it?

That is Noor's story.

Graceful, intelligent, and adored by a nation, she hides a secret ache: the belief that her parents' love was already perfect, already complete—that nothing she creates could ever compare.

And so, she chooses safety. Distance. Self-denial wrapped in quiet service.

Until a restoration architect named Rafi El-Zarif arrives to help repair a forgotten wing of the Celestial Sanctuary.

He is not of her world.

He does not kneel to legacy.

And he sees her not as a symbol—but as a woman filled with fierce potential and a hunger she's never dared voice.

Drawn together by ancient secrets, celestial ruins, and the pull of something deeper than gravity, Noor must confront her deepest fear: that love was never meant to be inherited. It was meant to be claimed.

And the stars...

they have something else in mind.

"Love is not a legacy we replicate—
it is a flame we awaken in our own way.
Not to imitate.
But to liberate."

Chapter One

The stones remembered everything.

Noor stepped lightly across the mosaic floor, where vines had begun to grow through the cracks of her mother's sanctuary. The archways, once etched with constellations, were worn now, faded by time, sun, and stories no one had told in years.

This was the Sky Wing—the eastern extension of Bayt al-Nujūm, the House of Stars, long since abandoned after a flood shifted the foundation and made it unsafe. A place her mother had once dreamed would house a library of sacred sky texts.

It had become a half-forgotten ruin.

Which, she supposed, made her a half-forgotten heir.

Noor crouched and brushed her fingers over a broken tile. Aldebaran's glyph. Worn almost smooth.

She closed her eyes.

She should have felt reverence.

Instead, she felt... pressure.

Everywhere she turned, she was reminded of it—their love. Celeste and Zayad. Her parents. Legends. Architects of peace, of light, of a nation reborn.

How could she dare to want something of her own? Something messy, uncertain, unscripted?

She stood and turned—then stopped.

He was there. Watching her.

A man in earth-toned linen, sleeves rolled, a dust-covered scarf slung over one shoulder. Skin sun-warmed, hair unruly, one brow slashed with an old scar that only made his gaze more unreadable.

He didn't look away.

Neither did she.

"Can I help you?" she asked, voice cool as desert glass.

He nodded toward the cracked archway behind her. "You're standing in the fracture line."

She stepped back without a word.

He crouched where she'd been, pulled a thin rod from his satchel, and tapped the stone gently.

It answered with a hollow sound.

"Eastern load-bearing wall's compromised," he said. "If we're going to save it, we'll need to reinforce beneath the third column. Soon."

"You speak like it matters."

He looked up. "Doesn't it?"

She didn't answer.

"You're Noor."

"And you are...?"

"Rafi El-Zarif. Restoration architect. Coastal Guild. I was summoned by your Council."

She folded her arms. "You weren't expected until tomorrow."

"I arrived early."

"Unannounced."

He shrugged. "The roof didn't wait. Why should I?"

A silence stretched between them—irritatingly comfortable.

Then he stood.

Something in her tightened. Not fear. Not attraction, exactly. Just… presence.

He didn't carry himself like the scholars or ministers she grew up around. He carried himself like someone who built things, whose hands knew how to shape what others called broken.

She hated how much that intrigued her.

"I'll need full access to the sanctuary," he said. "Including the archived blueprints."

"I'll consider it," she replied.

"You always begin with 'no'?"

"I always begin with caution."

He smiled then—just a ghost of it—but it disarmed something she hadn't meant to reveal.

"I like women who begin with caution," he said, already turning back to his tools.

Noor watched him go, the name Rafi El-Zarif echoing strangely in her mind.

She told herself it was nothing.

But the stars above—watching from their place just beyond the cracked dome—already knew better.

.   .   .

Coming Soon

EXCERPT STOLEN BY THE SHEIKH

CHAPTER ONE

Truth? Where did anyone even begin, Sheikh Anwar na Hassir questioned. In a world enamoured with lies, the truth seemed as impossible as the rarest sapphire in his Ceylonese mines to extract.

It begins with finding the woman who brought the curse of shame onto his family. Lucy Gaysford. Except she wasn't Lucy Gaysford any more, he growled, reading the shortened name emblazoned across the gallery window, signalling the solo exhibition by artist Lucy Ford. Anwar wrapped the gold New Zealand Merino scarf tighter around his neck, stealing himself to New York's wintery bite as he stood outside the Manhattan art gallery and glanced in.

She had been economical with the truth before. What other secrets was she now keeping?

Why had he come? In pursuit of truth and justice, he told himself, registering the kick of anticipation that trembled through his stomach as he caught a glimpse of his target. His eyes trailed her backless dress, revealing the sensuous curve of her spine as she wove through the crowd. A jolt of longing quivered through him.

Beauty, that's all, he cursed, forcing forbidden desire to a dull, barely perceivable tremor. Dammit. Why couldn't he shake the longing, the need—the pain of her betrayal?

Family honour, came the answer. To find the truth no matter the cost. He clenched his fist, bending his formidable will to his purpose. He would force from her the confession that her escape had invaded. He would silence the uneasy sense that he had been mistaken. That it was his beloved cousin who was the cause of so much hurt. That Hamad might've lied was untenable. Wasn't it better to accept the deceit of a Westerner, a woman with whom he had a short, passionate fling, rather than yield to the realisation that his own family had betrayed his love?

He paused before joining the intoxicated crowd inside, liquored up with complimentary drinks designed to adle their minds and open their wallets. He turned and glanced at the snow-lined streets festooned for the festive season. Thankfully, the gallery had not gone overboard with tawdry tinsel and garish, neon Christmas lights celebrating the birth of the Christian son his culture did not recognise but knew instead as God's prophet. Instead, as he redirected his attention indoors, he noticed with admiration that both unsettled and pleased him that the gallery was a shrine to love.

Love! He mused, noticing discomfort prickle his skin. What did he know of love? Oh yes—love of the inanimate. That was his refuge. Art, nature, his prized exotic orchids, and Zephyr, his loyal falcon, from whom he was rarely parted. These were the loves upon which he could rely.

He narrowed his formidable gaze in search of the woman he was here to make atone for the sin of her betrayal. He would extract her confession and then be done with Lucy, whatever her name was, forever.

. . .

AVAILABLE NOW—ebook, print, and audio. You'll find all the links and bonus videos on my website:

https://www.molliemathews.com/stolen-by-the-sheikh/

I hope you enjoyed reading about Anwar's older brother
Sheikh Tariq na Hassir. If you did, you'll enjoy his love story.

Read on for a free excerpt of this full length romance, Claimed by The Sheikh — is available in ebook, audio, paperback and hardcopy

CHAPTER ONE

"A re you trying to kill her?" Tariq na Hassir, the formidable ruler of the Kingdom of Avana, seized the animal handler's arm, forcing him to release the rope laced around the baby giraffe's neck.

"She has suffered enough trauma." Tariq dismissed the man with a fierce scowl that struck fear into enemies.

A slither of panic crept into the young man's hushed apology. "I am sorry, your Excellency."

"Release the others from their cages," Tariq growled.

The man did not have to be asked twice. He knew from experience that the Sheikh's retribution for disobedience would be swift and merciless.

"You are safe from harm," Tariq said softly, stroking the baby giraffe's long neck with a gentleness that belied his strength.

"No one will ever hurt you again, Noor," he said softly, impulsively naming her as his fingertips swept through the calf's fur. He let his long, supple fingers linger a moment upon her tail. Thankfully, they had saved her in time, he thought as he reached for the reins, clenching his powerful hands around the soft leather.

The rage he had first felt on hearing about the ruthless murder of the newborn's mother still roared through him. Had she been executed to pay a tail dowry to the father of some money-mongering bride, he wondered? Or did some heinous person pay thousands of dollars for a wretched fly swatter?

Noor looked up and met Tariq's dark gaze. In her innocent eyes, he saw her despair, her disillusionment, her disgust with humanity. He recognized her trauma as though it was his own. Because it was.

"Humans," he said, his voice marinated with contempt. "The people you should be able to trust, the people who say they care, the people whose actions should be driven by love —the majority are driven by nothing but selfishness, deception, and lies."

Taking a bottle of milk, he placed the teat to Noor's lips. The calf's silky black lashes grazed her cheeks as she gazed down at the foreign object and then looked back at Tariq. She stared silently up at him, her eyes moist and bewildered.

Tariq had trained himself to shut down his emotions, but that skill suddenly failed him. His chest trembled with suppressed rage, knowing the orphaned baby would never again taste her mother's milk.

"What passes for love among some people is abhorrent," he said in a low, strained voice. "On behalf of humanity, I apologize."

The killing of the calf's mother and three other rare Kordofan giraffes by trophy hunters seeking their tails further motivated the Sheikh's commitment to transform his anger into action.

"Do you really think you can save her?"

Tariq looked at Anwar, his younger brother by 11 months.

His head was slightly bowed, but he could see his eyes were fixed in sadness and longing.

Tension ripped down Tariq's spine. "Our father's reign of terror and tyranny have robbed Avana of prosperity and peace. I will make it my personal mission to right the injustices of the past. War and hostility must end. And it starts with how we treat those most vulnerable."

His fingers shook as he gripped the bottle of milk as Noor, at last, began to suckle.

An eerie silence swept across the precipitous landscape of Avana's Tiwa oasis. Tariq lifted his gaze to the horizon. The only movement visible to his naked eye was the wind etching a delicate furrow as it crawled over the golden dunes.

"Not only will I provide a sanctuary for hunted wildlife and orphans like Noor, but I will liberate God's most precious creatures from the many closing zoos and other inhumane habitats around the world," he glanced over at the other animals being unloaded from the custom-built crates.

"I will create a world-acclaimed sanctuary, impenetrable by those with impure and malicious hearts. It will be the most magical, marvelous, mesmerizingly unique place, the number one eco-tourism destination in the world. I will create meaningful employment for our people, restoring their dignity, attracting millions of visitors annually, and contributing billions to the economy. But more importantly, I will show the world how kindness and compassion can be turned into plutonium and change the world."

Anwar glanced at the now lush landscape and recalled how barren it had once been. With no sign of life in sight, others had found it impossible to fathom his brother's vision to transform the punishing and unforgiving conditions into a haven for so many endangered species. Yet, as with everything Tariq turned his formidable will and mind-blowing wealth to, he had succeeded where mere mortals were destined to fail.

Anwar's heart swelled with pride as he thought of all his brother's achievements. "It's an audacious and admirable plan. And if anyone can pull it off, it's you, brother. Your passion, your drive, your unrelenting ambition, and your pursuit of goals exceed mere mortals. And you have the endurance and power of 13,000 Arabian horses, but aren't you setting yourself up for too much hard work? Why don't you relax? Kick back. Enjoy the fruits of your reign?" Anwar said, tossing his head in the direction of the harem. "Other men would."

"Women were our father's weakness," bitterness bled from his words. "I, too, once made the same mistake. I, too, paid the price."

There was a tense silence while Tariq lifted his gaze to the sky and studied the giant falcon circling above.

"Was it not you who once taught that your greatest weakness can also be your greatest strength?" Anwar asked.

Tariq shook his head, biting down a terse retort. "I was misled." He said, nodding his command to the animal handler lingering at a respectful distance.

He petted Noor as she was led away. "All kinds of atrocities are committed in the name of love, which is why it is the most dangerous of emotions and why I am forever turned off to women."

AVAILABLE NOW—ebook, print, and audio. You'll find all the links and bonus videos on my website:
https://www.molliemathews.com/claimed-by-the-sheikh/

. . .

If you enjoyed meeting lipstick designer Poppy Pac, you'll love her and Ethan's special love story in the full-length book *For The Love of Lipstick.*

Keep reading for a sneak peek.

Let passion provide the ultimate escape…
the *Montana Brides* series, where it's never too late to find love
Coming soon!

EXCERPT: FOR THE LOVE OF LIPSTICK

If my own mother doesn't love me, who will?

44-year-old Poppy Pac sat alone in her dimly lit living room, surrounded by a sea of tissues and the lingering scent of sorrow. Her beloved husband, James, had passed away just a month ago, leaving behind an emptiness that seemed impossible to fill. As a mortgage broker, Poppy had always been the strong and capable one, guiding others through the complexities of homeownership. But now, she felt lost and adrift in a world that no longer made sense.

She had spent her life trying not to be noticed, deferring to her husband, who was content to write poetry, while she worked diligently in a shadow career, in part to avoid her mother's envy. But now James was gone—and her mother offered no comfort.

Her best friend, Lizzie, knew that Poppy needed something to pour her grief into, something that would ignite her passion and bring a glimmer of light back into her life.

. . .

The next afternoon, Lily arrived at Poppy's doorstep carrying a bag filled with an array of colorful pigments, waxes, and oils.

"Poppy," Lily said gently, her voice filled with empathy, "I know how much you loved making things. Remember when we used to spend hours crafting together? "Do you remember the fun we had brewing lip gloss on the kitchen stove and pouring it into bottle caps for sale at school? I know it was a long time ago; but I thought maybe, just maybe, pouring your grief into your hobby of making lipstick could help heal your heart."

Poppy looked up, her eyes red and puffy from countless tears. She reached for a tissue and dabbed at her eyes, contemplating Lily's suggestion. Making lipstick had always been a passion of hers—a creative outlet that allowed her to express herself in a unique and vibrant way. But since James's passing, she had abandoned her hobby, feeling as though there was no joy left in her life.

Lily gently placed the bag of lipstick-making supplies on the coffee table, her eyes filled with hope. "I brought every-thing you need to get started. Remember how much fun we had experimenting with different shades and textures? Maybe, just maybe, rediscovering that joy could bring a spark back into your world."

Poppy stared at the bag, her mind swirling with a mixture of longing and uncertainty. Could something as simple as making lipstick really help her heal? She glanced at Lily, her friend's unwavering support shining through her eyes.

Taking a deep breath, Poppy nodded. "Okay, Lily. Let's give it a try. Maybe it's time to pour my grief into something beautiful."

Lily's face lit up with a smile, and together, they opened the bag, revealing a treasure trove of colors and possibilities.

They cleared the coffee table, making space for their creative endeavor, and Poppy felt a flicker of excitement deep within her soul.

"Do you remember that crazy mixture we made, melting down all our leftover lipsticks? It was such a beautiful shade. I wish I still had it," Poppy said, pressing her fingers to her nude lips. "I called it "Happiness" because I always felt so wonderful when I wore it." Her thoughts drifted back to James. She'd be wearing *Happiness* when they first met.

"Maybe we can make it again," Lily said as they began carefully selecting pigments and mixing and blending them to create a palette of emotions.

Poppy didn't know if she would find happiness again, but she found solace in the rhythmic stirring of the blend, losing herself in the swirls of color that danced before her eyes. With each stroke of the spatula, she felt a small part of her grief being transformed into something tangible and beautiful.

As they added waxes and oils, the mixture took on a soft and velvety texture, much like the touch of James' hand on her cheek. Poppy closed her eyes, allowing the familiar scent of vanilla and lavender to envelop her senses. At that moment, she felt a deep connection to her husband, as if he was guiding her hands and whispering words of encouragement.

With Lily's guidance, Poppy poured the mixture into small lipstick molds, watching as the liquid transformed into solid pillars of color. As they waited for the lipsticks to set, they shared stories of James, their laughter mingling with tears of remembrance.

Finally, the lipsticks were ready, each one a unique reflection of Poppy's journey through grief. She carefully wrapped them in delicate tissue paper, feeling a renewed sense of purpose and a glimmer of hope.

Days turned into weeks, and Poppy found herself creating more and more lipsticks. Each one became a testament to her strength and resilience, a tiny vessel of healing that she could share with others. As she applied the lipstick to her own lips, she felt a sense of empowerment, a reminder that she could still find beauty in a world that had seemed so dark after James' death.

COMING SOON!

BY MOLLIE MATHEWS

THE SHEIKHS UNTAMED BRIDES

CLAIMED BY THE SHEIKH
STOLEN BY THE SHEIKH
BOUGHT BY THE SHEIKH
FORGOTTEN BY THE SHEIKH
UNTAMED BY THE SHEIKH
UNVEILED BY THE SHEIKH
DECEIVED BY THE SHEIKH
THE SHEIKHS UNTAMED BRIDES BOX SET BOOKS 1-2
THE SHEIKHS UNTAMED BRIDES BOX SET BOOKS 1-3
THE SHEIKHS UNTAMED BRIDES BOX SET BOOKS 1-5

GEMSTONE BILLIONAIRES

THE ITALIAN BILLIONAIRE'S CHRISTMAS BRIDE

THE ITALIAN BILLIONAIRE'S SCANDALOUS
MARRIAGE
THE ITALIAN BILLIONAIRE'S SAPPHIRE BRIDE
THE ITALIAN BILLIONAIRE'S LEGACY OF LOVE
GEMSTONE BILLIONAIRES 2 BOOK-BUNDLE
BOX SET
GEMSTONE BILLIONAIRES 3 BOOK-BUNDLE
BOX SET

TRUE LOVE

LOVE IN VENICE (3rd place winner Koru Award)
LOVE IN MEXICO
LOVE IN SICILY
LOVE IN MONTANA
LOVE IN TUSCANY
LOVE IN GREECE
LOVE IN SANTORINI

MONTANA HEARTS
A CHRISTMAS OF HER OWN
EVERLASTING CHRISTMAS

MONTANA COZY ART MYSTERIES
MURDER ON THE CANVAS
MURDER IN THE FRAME
MONTANA COZY ART MYSTERIES 2 BOOK-BUNDLE
BOX SET

NASHVILLE HEARTS

ONE STEP AT A TIME
LOVE RISING

PASSION DOWN UNDER SASSY SHORT STORIES

TWIST OF FATE
LOVE ME FOREVER
FOREVER AND ALWAYS
LOVE ME AS I AM
THE LIGHTKEEPER'S LOVER
FINDING A HUSBAND
LOVE ALL OF ME
CRAZY FOR YOU

PASSION DOWN UNDER 2 BOOK-BUNDLE BOX SET
(Books 1 & 2)
PASSION DOWN UNDER 3 BOOK-BUNDLE BOX SET
(Books 1, 2 & 3)
PASSION DOWN UNDER 6 BOOK-BUNDLE BOX SET

SHORT, SWEET SHEIKH LOVE STORIES
DESTINY
LUCKY

BITTERSWEET LOVE STORIES
WHAT IS SOFT IS STRONG

NASHVILLE HEARTS

ONE STEP AT A TIME
LOVE RISING

FLOURISHING HEARTS
THE GIRL IN PINK SKATES

ABOUT THE AUTHOR

MOLLIE MATHEWS is an award-winning artist and author known for her "sensual, beautiful, empowered stories enveloped in true romance" (Amazon review) and characters who feel real.

Whether they be Italian billionaires, handsome sheikhs, maverick cowboys, empowered heroines, or everyday people, readers of Mollie's romances say she "is a beyond compelling storyteller with the gift and the power to make you experience her remarkable craft on a whole other level."

She lives in the idyllic Bay of Islands, New Zealand, on a rural property overlooking the sea. There, surrounded by nature's beauty and inspiration, she writes her love stories. She also follows the sun, dividing her time between New

Zealand and exotic locations—wherever she intends to set her next romance novel. She lives with her romantic hero, Lorenzo—tall, dark, terribly handsome, and fluent in Spanish!

Mollie passionately believes books are medicine and the power of romance to transform people's lives. Her stories are unashamedly positive, hopeful, and optimistic. Despite the struggles and obstacles the people in her stories face, they are always rewarded with love and the happily ever after of their dreams.

Happy reading xxx

ISBN eBook: 978-1-991374-13-4

ISBN print: 978-1-991374-14-1

ISBN audio: 978-1-991374-15-8

Published by

Blue Orchid Publishing New Zealand

Blue Orchid
PUBLISHING

Visit www.molliemathews.com to read more about all our books and to buy them. You will also find features, author interviews and news of author events, and you can sign up for e-newsletters so that you're always first to hear about our new releases.